Alex Thom

Irish Land Commission under Land Purchase Acts, March 1897

Rules, Forms, Directions and Schedule of Fees

Alex Thom

Irish Land Commission under Land Purchase Acts, March 1897
Rules, Forms, Directions and Schedule of Fees

ISBN/EAN: 9783742802521

Manufactured in Europe, USA, Canada, Australia, Japa

Cover: Foto ©Andreas Hilbeck / pixelio.de

Manufactured and distributed by brebook publishing software
(www.brebook.com)

Alex Thom

Irish Land Commission under Land Purchase Acts, March 1897

LAND PURCHASE ACTS.

RULES, FORMS, DIRECTIONS, AND SCHEDULE OF FEES

ISSUED BY THE

IRISH LAND COMMISSION.

16th day of March, 1897.

Presented to Parliament by Command of Her Majesty.

DUBLIN:

PRINTED FOR HER MAJESTY'S STATIONERY OFFICE,

BY ALEX. THOM & CO. (LIMITED), ABBEY-STREET.

And to be purchased, either directly or through any Bookseller, from
HODGES, FIGGIS, and Co. (LIMITED), 104, Grafton-street, Dublin; or
EYRE and SPOTTISWOODE, East Harding-street, Fleet-street, E.C.; or
JOHN MENZIES and Co., 12, Hanover-street, Edinburgh, and
90, West Nile-street, Glasgow.

1897.

[C.—8390.]   *Price* 5½*d.*

CONTENTS.

ORDERS.

Number.	Subject Matter.	Page.
I.	Construction of terms,	7
II.	Examiners and Registrar,	8
III.	Time,	8
IV.	Originating Statement,	8
V.	Notices and Requisitions to Quit Rent Office and Board of Public Works, and Requisition as to Tithe-rentcharge,	11
VI.	Lis Pendens,	11
VII.	Appearances,	12
VIII.	Services,	13
IX.	Lodgment and Delivery of Deeds, &c.,	14
X.	Abstract of Title,	16
XI.	Rulings on Title, and ascertainment of Superior Interests,	16
XII.	Agreement for Purchase and Application for an Advance,	17
XIII.	Maps and Surveys,	18
XIV.	Inspection of Holding,	20
XV.	Conditional sanction of advance or agreement for purchase; notification to parties,	20
XVI.	Vesting Order,	21
XVII.	Proof of Occupancy,	23
XVIII.	Making of advance and Charging Order,	23
XIX.	Registration of Purchaser's ownership,	24
XX.	Apportionment and Redemption of Superior Interests,	25
XXI.	Allocation,	28
XXII.	Investments,	31
XXIII.	Guarantee Deposits,	31
XXIV.	Payment into Bank of Ireland under Sec. 14 of the Land Law (Ireland) Act, 1887,	33
XXV.	Appointment of Trustees,	34
XXVI.	Partition and Exchange,	35
XXVII.	Specific performance,	36
XXVIII.	Change of parties by death, &c.,	36
XXIX.	Persons under disability,	36
XXX.	Motions and Orders,	37
XXXI.	Cause against Conditional Order,	39
XXXII.	Evidence and Examination of Witnesses,	39
XXXIII.	Affidavits,	41
XXXIV.	Sequestration and Attachment,	42
XXXV.	Questions of Law and Appeals,	48
XXXVI.	Sale by a Landlord to a Tenant in consideration of a fine and a rentcharge,	44
XXXVII.	Purchase by a Tenant from the Land Judges,	45

Number.	Subject Matter.	Page.
XXXVIII.	Purchase of estates by the Land Commission for resale, and negotiations of Sales by the Land Commission,	45
XXXIX.	Sales under section 40 of the Land Law (Ireland) Act, 1896,	46
XL.	Preliminary Expenses,	46
XLI.	Proceedings under the Redemption of Rent (Ireland) Act, 1891,	47
XLII.	Entitling and filing of Documents,	49
XLIII.	Certified Copies and Production of Documents,	49
XLIV.	Solicitors,	50
XLV.	Delay in conduct of proceedings,	50
XLVI.	Costs,	51
XLVII.	Proceedings for Recovery of Costs,	53
XLVIII.	Order to Sheriff to put Purchaser into possession,	53
XLIX.	Application that Annuity be not reduced at end of decade,	54
L.	Retention of Land Certificate by Land Commission,	54
LL.	Letters on official business,	54

APPENDIX.

FORMS.

Number.	Subject Matter.	Page.
1	Originating Statement,	55
2	Notice of the Filing of an Originating Statement,	59
3	General Notice to Claimants,	60
4	Notice and Requisition to Quit Rent Office,	61
5	Notice and Requisition to Board of Public Works,	62
6	Requisition as to Tithe Rentcharge,	63
7	Certificate for registering a Lis Pendens,	64
8	General Certificate of Appearances,	65
9	Certificate of the entry of an Appearance,	65
10	Agreement for Sale between Vendor and Tenant,	66
11	Notice to lodge Deeds, &c.,	70
12	Affidavit verifying Abstract of Title,	70
13	Draft Requisition for Searches in the Registry of Deeds,	71
14	Direction for Survey by Ordnance Survey Department,	71
15	Affidavit verifying Occupancy,	72
16	Application for the apportionment of Tithe Rentcharge payable to the Land Commission,	73
17	Application for the apportionment of Fixed Annual Instalments in lieu of Tithe Rentcharge,	75
18	Statement of Facts for the apportionment of an Impropriate Tithe Rentcharge,	77

Number.	Subject Matter.	Page.
19	Statement of Facts for the apportionment of Quit or Crown Rent,	78
20	Statement of Facts for the apportionment of Rent, Fees, Duties, or Services,	80
21	Statement of Facts for the apportionment of a Rent-charge or an Annuity,	82
22	Request to appoint an Arbitrator,	84
23	Submission to Arbitration and Appointment of Arbitrators and Umpire,	85
24	Award,	86
25	Allocation Schedule,	87
26	Privity for the lodgment of a Guarantee Deposit,	87
27	Notice of Motion to appoint Trustees for the purposes of the Settled Land Acts, 1882 to 1890,	88
28	Statement of Facts for the appointment of Trustees under Sec. 00 of the Landed Estates Court Act,	88
29	Notice of lodgment of Surveyor's Report and Scheme for Partition,	89
30	Commission to examine Witnesses,	90
31	Summons for the attendance of Witnesses and for the production of Documents,	90
32	Writ of Sequestration,	91
33	Requisition to have the Order of a Commissioner not made upon a Question of Law reconsidered by a Judicial Commissioner and two other Commissioners,	91
34	Application by a Tenant for an advance to enable him to purchase his holding from the Land Judges,	92
35	Undertaking by Tenant to purchase his holding from the Land Commission, and Application for Advance,	93
36	Application by a Landlord to the Land Commission to purchase his estate for resale,	94
37	Originating Notice under the Redemption of Rent (Ireland) Act, 1891,	95
38	Consent to Redemption under the Redemption of Rent (Ireland) Act, 1891,	96
39	Notice of lodgment of Consent to Redemption,	97
40	Application for an advance under the Redemption of Rent (Ireland) Act, 1891,	97
41	Notice of Conditional Order for redemption under the Redemption of Rent (Ireland) Act, 1891,	99
42	Certificate to register Apprentice or Clerk,	99
43	Certificate of registration of Apprentice or Clerk,	100
44	Writ of Fieri Facias for costs,	100
45	Affidavit to ground application for order for possession,	101
46	Order to Sheriff to put Purchaser into possession,	101
	DIRECTIONS AS TO THE PREPARATION OF ABSTRACTS OF TITLE,	102
	DIRECTIONS AS TO THE PREPARATION OF AFFIDAVITS UNDER ORDER XX., r. 16,	103
	SCHEDULE OF FEES,	105

IRISH LAND COMMISSION.

RULES

UNDER

THE LAND PURCHASE ACTS.

16th day of March, 1897.

It is this day ordered that the following General Rules and Orders shall, from and after this date and until further order, take effect and be in force in the Irish Land Commission in relation to all proceedings under and in pursuance of the Land Purchase Acts as defined by the Land Law (Ireland) Act, 1896, and that all Rules and Orders, except the Rules dated this day in relation to proceedings under Part V. of the said Act, shall cease to be in force as regards all proceedings commenced or continued after this date; save that as regards proceedings now pending, where these Rules and Orders are not applicable, the general Rules and Orders in force at the date hereof shall remain in force as if these Rules had not been made.

ORDER I.

CONSTRUCTION OF TERMS.

1. In these Rules, unless the context otherwise requires, "Land Commission" shall mean Irish Land Commission; "Commissioner" shall mean one of the Irish Land Commissioners; "the Judicial Commissioner" shall mean the Judicial Commissioner of the Land Commission; "a Judicial Commissioner" shall include the Land Judge of the Chancery Division of the High Court of Justice in Ireland; "a Land Judge" shall include the Judicial Commissioner of the Land Commission when acting as a Land Judge; "High Court" shall mean Her Majesty's High Court of Justice in Ireland; "Court" shall mean Court of the Irish Land Commission; "holiday" shall mean any day upon which the offices of the Land Commission shall be closed; "the Commissioner," and "the Examiner" shall respectively mean the Commissioner or Examiner to whom the proceeding in question is for the time being referred; and all other expressions shall have the meaning assigned to them by the Land Purchase Acts.

ORDER II.

EXAMINERS AND REGISTRAR.

1. The Examiners and Registrar shall perform their respective duties in person; provided that when any Rule or Order directs that any act shall be done, or duty discharged by an Examiner, or by the Registrar, the same may be done or discharged, in the case of an Examiner, by the First Assistant Examiner, or an Assistant Examiner, with the sanction of the Judicial Commissioner; and in the case of the Registrar, by such officer as the Judicial Commissioner shall for that purpose from time to time appoint.

ORDER III.

TIME.

1. In the computation of time for the purpose of these Rules and Orders, the word "month" shall mean calendar month, and the period of a month shall not be extended by reason of any intervening holiday, but when the time limited is a fortnight or any less period, the time so limited shall be extended by any intervening holiday or holidays except Sundays.

2. The computation of time by days shall be exclusive of the first and inclusive of the last day.

3. Whenever the time limited expires on a Sunday or other holiday it shall be extended to the next day on which the offices of the Land Commission shall be open.

4. The Court shall have power to enlarge or abridge the time appointed by these Rules and Orders, or fixed by any Order, for doing any act, or taking any proceedings, upon such terms, if any, as the justice of the case may require, and any such enlargement may be applied for and ordered after the expiration of the time appointed or allowed.

ORDER IV.

ORIGINATING STATEMENT.

Proceedings to be commenced by originating statement.

1. All proceedings for sale under the Land Purchase Acts shall, unless the sale be by the Land Judges, be commenced by the lodgment of an originating statement.

Form, and verification of.

2. The statement shall be in accordance with Form I, in the Appendix hereto, with such variations as the nature of the case may require, or in such other form as the Land Commission may from time to time direct. It shall be fairly written on post paper, book-wise, with sufficient margin, and with a parchment back, shall be divided into paragraphs, and shall be verified by the affidavit of the vendor or vendors, or, if a Commissioner shall so permit, by the vendor's solicitor, who shall state in the affidavit

the reason why the statement is verified by him and not by the vendor. The person verifying the statement shall, before making his affidavit, make all reasonable inquiries to ascertain what superior interests as defined by section 31 of the Land Law (Ireland) Act, 1896 (if any) affect the lands.

3. The statement shall include all lands which the vendor intends to sell, and any of his lands upon which his tenants have rights of grazing or turbary, and, if the vendor intends selling part only of any townland, the statement shall include the entire of such townland, or so much thereof as belongs to the vendor. The statement may include all lands which are held by the vendor under a common, or partly common title, or which are subject to any common incumbrance, but the vendor may, if he so desire, insert a statement after the name of any townland to the effect that the same, or any particular part thereof, is excluded from the proceedings. The Ordnance Survey names only of the townlands shall be used in the originating statement, and if the estate comprises part only of a townland it must be so stated.

Lands to be included in.

4. No originating statement shall be lodged comprising any land in respect of which proceedings for sale, or for declaration of title, are pending before the Land Judges.

Not to include lands the subject matter of proceedings before the Land Judges.

5. When a person desires to sell under the Land Purchase Acts land comprised in an originating statement already lodged, the former vendor's interest in which he shall have acquired by purchase or otherwise before such vendor had agreed to sell such land to the tenant or tenants thereof, such person or his solicitor shall, before lodging an originating statement, take the Examiner's direction as to its preparation, with a view to avoiding the repetition of matter disclosed by the statement already lodged, or in the course of the proceedings in the former matter, and as to how far the abstract of title and other documents already lodged may be utilised in the new proceedings. The statement, when lodged, shall be referred to the Commissioner to whom the statement and proceedings in the former matter stood referred.

Directions where land is to be sold is included in an originating statement already filed by another person.

6. Each originating statement shall be endorsed with the name, and registered place of business of the vendor's solicitor, or, if the vendor is not represented by a solicitor, with an address within the municipal boundary of the city of Dublin to be called the vendor's address for service, where notices, orders, and other documents may be left for him.

Statement to be endorsed with vendor's address for service, or the name and address of his solicitor.

7. The statement shall be filed in the Registrar's office, and the Registrar shall endorse thereon the date of filing. Every statement shall be marked with the record number indicating the order in which it has been received, shall be entered in the index of cases and record of proceedings, and shall be referred to such Commissioner, and in such rotation as the Land Commission may from time to time direct, and all subsequent proceedings usually conducted before one Commissioner shall,

Filing, and reference to a Commissioner.

save as may be otherwise directed by rule, be conducted before the Commissioner to whom the statement has been referred; provided that the statement and proceedings, or any matter arising thereunder may at any time be transferred on the fiat of the Judicial Commissioner from any one Commissioner to another, and on transfer of the statement and proceedings the minutes on the index of cases and record of proceedings shall be altered accordingly.

Amendment of originating statement. 8. No amendment shall be made in any originating statement that has been filed except by leave of the Commissioner, and in such manner as he may direct, and every such amendment shall be initialled and dated by the Registrar.

Supplemental statement. 9. Additional statements, when lodged, shall be deemed to be supplemental to, and shall be endorsed with the record number of the originating statement and with a distinguishing letter. When, however, a vendor who has already lodged an originating statement desires to institute proceedings for the sale of additional lands, the title to, and incumbrances (if any) upon which are in no way common with the title to, or incumbrances upon the lands comprised in any originating statement already filed by him, the Commissioner may, if it shall appear to him expedient having regard to the special circumstances of the case, permit an originating statement to be lodged, and to receive a new record number.

Notice of filing, and general notice to claimants. 10. The originating statement, when filed, shall be laid before the Commissioner, who shall endorse thereon directions as to the service of the notice of filing, the publication of the general notice to claimants, the payment of interest on the purchase money, and such other matters as he may think fit. The notice of filing shall be in Form 2, or such other form as the Commissioner may direct. Subject to any directions that may be given by the Commissioner, it shall be served upon all persons named in the originating statement as entitled to any superior interest or incumbrance affecting the lands (except Her Majesty the Queen, the Commissioners of Public Works in Ireland, or the Land Commission). The general notice to claimants shall be in Form 3.

Proceedings when originating statement in accordance with Rules, dated 15th August, 1891, has been lodged. 11. When the vendor has lodged an originating statement in accordance with the General Rules dated 15th August, 1891, it shall not be necessary for him, unless the Commissioner shall otherwise direct, to lodge any further originating statement in respect of land therein comprised; but, before lodging any agreement for purchase, the vendor or his solicitor shall attend before the Examiner, and take his directions as to the further proceedings. If the Examiner be satisfied that there is no superior interest affecting the land which would necessitate further service of the notice of filing, or further publication, he shall endorse on the originating statement a certificate to that effect, and the agreement for purchase may thereupon be lodged. If it shall appear to the Examiner that further service or publication is necessary, he shall lay the originating statement before the Commissioner for directions, and, before doing so, he may require the vendor to furnish such further evidence by affidavit or otherwise as may be necessary.

ORDER V.

NOTICES AND REQUISITIONS TO THE QUIT RENT OFFICE AND BOARD OF PUBLIC WORKS, AND REQUISITION AS TO TITHE-RENTCHARGE.

1. Together with the originating statement there shall be lodged in duplicate for transmission through the Notice Office notices and requisitions to the Quit Rent Office and Board of Public Works in Forms 4 and 5. There shall also be lodged a requisition as to tithe-rentcharge in Form 6. *To be lodged with originating statement.*

2. The notices and requisitions shall include all the lands comprised in the originating statement, and if part only of any townland be included, the words "part of" must be inserted before the name of such townland. *Shall include all lands in statement.*

3. The vendor or his solicitor shall be responsible for the accuracy of the notices and requisitions, and if any of them be found to be inaccurate in any particular, the costs thereof may be disallowed on taxation. *Vendor, or his solicitor to be responsible for accuracy of.*

4. It shall be the duty of the vendor or his solicitor to furnish to the Quit Rent Office and Board of Public Works respectively such documents and other evidence as may be necessary to enable them to comply with the requisitions. *Vendor, or his solicitor to furnish documents and evidence.*

5. As soon as the returns to such requisitions have been made and noted, the requisitions, with the returns endorsed, shall be transmitted to the vendor or his solicitor. *Returns to requisitions.*

ORDER VI.

LIS PENDENS.

As soon as the originating statement has been filed, the vendor or his solicitor shall register the matter as a *lis pendens*, and the Registrar shall, if so required, sign a certificate of the filing of the originating statement for this purpose in Form 7.

ORDER VII.

APPEARANCES.

1. An "Appearance Book" shall be kept in the Registrar's Office in which any person claiming to be interested in the subject matter of any proceedings shall be at liberty, either personally or by his solicitor, to enter an appearance for the purpose of being served with notice of such proceedings; and any person so appearing may withdraw his appearance.

2. If a person appears by a solicitor, the name and registered place of business of such solicitor shall be stated. If the appearance be not by a solicitor, the person appearing shall give an address within the municipal boundary of the city of Dublin where notices may be left for him; and such address may be altered by him from time to time.

3. An appearance may be either general for the purpose of receiving notice of all proceedings in the matter, or special in order that the person appearing may have notice of any particular proceeding to be therein specified, or for the purpose of giving a consent or otherwise binding the party. The appearance, if general, must state whether the person appearing requires notice of the conditional sanction of all sales.

4. If the Commissioner considers that an appearance, whether general or special, has been entered without sufficient cause, he may direct such appearance to be cancelled, or he may direct a general appearance to be varied to a special one; and he may order the person appearing without sufficient cause, or entering a general appearance when a special appearance would have been sufficient, to pay the costs of any notice or other document that may have been served upon such person.

5. Every person entering, or withdrawing an appearance, or altering his address for service, shall give notice thereof in writing to the vendor or his solicitor; and no second or other appearance by any person in any one matter shall be permitted until the previous appearance be withdrawn.

6. All appearances shall be entered in the appearance book accurately and in a legible hand in the presence of the officer in charge of the book, whose duty it shall be to see that the proper notices are served.

7. The Registrar, or an officer of his department, shall, if required, sign a certificate in Form 8, specifying the appearances that shall have been entered in any matter, or a certificate in Form 9 of the entry of any particular appearance.

8. The vendor's address for service, or, if he be represented by a solicitor, the name and registered place of business of such solicitor shall be entered upon the record of proceedings.

9. Should the vendor desire to change his address for service, or his solicitor, or to appear in person, notice of the change shall be served upon the solicitor (if any), whose name appears on record as representing the vendor, and upon all persons who have entered appearances in the matter, and thereupon the entry on the record of proceedings shall be varied.

(margin: Change of solicitor or address by vendor.)

ORDER VIII.

SERVICES.

1. Any vendor or purchaser who has made or joined in any application to the Land Commission, and any person who has entered a general or special appearance in a matter may be served with any order or notice in the matter through the Notice Office of the Land Commission ; and any person who has served a notice of motion may be served in the same manner with any order or notice having relation to such notice of motion ; and any person who has been served with a conditional order, and against whom such order has been made absolute, may be served in the same manner with any order or notice.

(margin: Persons who may be served through Notice Office.)

2. Except in the cases aforesaid, any person whom it may be necessary to serve with any order or notice must be served personally, or at his residence, unless the Commissioner authorizes some other mode of service.

(margin: Other service to be personal, or at the residence.)

3. Service at the residence must be at the residence where the party is residing at the time, and should be upon the wife, husband, father, mother, son, daughter, brother or sister, or domestic servant of the party intended to be served. The person to whom the document is delivered must be of the age of sixteen years or upwards, and must be requested to give such document to the person for whom the same is intended. Service at a place of business shall not be deemed service at the residence.

(margin: What constituted service at the residence.)

4. In the case of any order, notice, or other document sealed or signed by an officer of the Court, the original should be shown unless it shall appear that such a course would be impracticable from the fact that parties residing far apart had to be served within a limited period.

(margin: Original to be shown except in certain cases.)

5. Every person requiring to have a notice or other document served through the Notice Office, shall, before the hour of two o'clock in the afternoon, or, if the day be a Saturday, before noon, leave with the proper officer the document which he shall require to have so served, together with as many copies thereof as he shall require to have served, and in the case of a notice of motion, two copies thereof for the use of the Court. The document required to be served, and also the copies thereof left for the use of the Court, shall have written at foot thereof or endorsed thereon the name and registered place of business of each solicitor, and the

(margin: Method of service through Notice Office.)

14

address for service of each party appearing in person on whom the same is to be served, and in the case of a solicitor the name of the party for whom he has appeared. There shall also be left at the same time envelopes directed to the several persons to be served at the several registered places of business and addresses for service endorsed on the document to be served. The person requiring the document to be served, or his solicitor, shall mark upon every copy thereof which he shall require to have served, and also upon each copy left for the use of the Court that the same has been compared with and is a true copy of the document required to be so served, and shall sign the same with his name or the initial letters thereof, and every such person or solicitor shall be responsible for the accuracy of every such copy.

Duty of the Officer receiving the notice.

6. The officer shall compare and check the addresses on the several envelopes with the names and addresses on the document to be served, and see that they correspond, and place the copies for service in their respective envelopes and secure the same, and place them with the official letters to be despatched the same day, and he shall enter in the register of notices a minute of the despatch of such copies and mark the entry with his initials. The originals of all documents transmitted through the Notice Office shall be filed, except in the case of a notice, or other document sealed or signed by an officer of the Court which may be retained by the person requiring the same to be served, provided he lodges a copy for filing.

Certificate of Officer to be proof of service through Notice Office.

7. Where any notice or other document is served through the Notice Office, the certificate of the proper officer that such notice or other document was duly transmitted by post shall be proof of the service thereof.

Substituted service.

8. Every application for an order for substituted, or other service, or for the substitution of notice for service, shall be supported by an affidavit setting forth the grounds upon which the application is made. Whenever any such order shall be made, a copy thereof shall be served along with the notice or other document, as the case may be.

Notices and other documents to be printed if six or more copies are required.

9. Every notice or other document of which six or more copies are required must be printed.

<hr>

ORDER IX.

LODGMENT AND DELIVERY OF DEEDS, &c.

Method of lodgment.

1. Deeds, muniments of title, and other documents directed to be lodged in Court, either in pursuance of General Rules and Orders, or of an order or ruling made in any matter, shall, unless otherwise directed, be lodged in the Record Office of the Land Commission, and the person lodging the same shall bring in two

schedules of such documents, one of which will be returned to him receipted by the Keeper of Records. If the documents are being lodged in pursuance of a notice or order, a copy of such notice or order must be produced at the time of the lodgment.

2. Any person having the custody of any deed or document relating to lands the subject matter of proceedings before the Land Commission, shall, if so ordered, and on such terms as the Court may think just, produce or lodge the same in Court for the purposes of such proceedings.

3. A mortgagee or a person entitled to a superior interest shall not be obliged to part with the instruments creating his security, or dealing with it, until the order for payment of his demand is made; but he shall be bound in the meantime to furnish copies thereof, if required, on payment of the ordinary charges, and to produce the originals if required by order of a Commissioner, or if the Examiner shall certify that such instruments are required for the vouching of the abstract of title.

4. The Court may make such order as may be just, as to the lien of any person lodging deeds, muniments of title, or other documents, or as to payment of the costs of lodging the same.

5. Before applying for an order upon any person to lodge deeds or other documents, notice must be served upon such person in Form 11, with such variations as the circumstances of the case may require; and when making the application there must be produced evidence that the person against whom the order is sought has the documents required in his custody, power, or procurement, and a certificate from the Keeper of Records that such documents have not been lodged.

6. Any solicitor or other person who is ordered to lodge deeds or other documents in Court shall, if he claims to have a lien on such documents, file an affidavit stating the particulars of such lien, and refer to such affidavit in the schedule of documents lodged, otherwise the lien may be disallowed.

7. Any person failing without sufficient cause to lodge in Court documents in his possession, power, or procurement, relating to lands the subject matter of proceedings before the Land Commission, within ten days of the service upon him of the notice referred to in Rule 5 of this Order, may be made liable for the costs of any application to the Court that may become necessary by reason of his default.

8. The Examiners shall have authority to order the delivery of documents lodged in the Record Office, on an undertaking to return the same being given, or finally, but the Examiner shall, if he thinks necessary, direct notice of an application for such

order to be given. They may also give any person whom they may consider entitled to do so liberty to inspect any documents so lodged. The Keeper of Records shall not, save as aforesaid, or save to an officer of the Land Commission, deliver any deeds or documents except by Order of the Commissioner.

ORDER X.

ABSTRACT OF TITLE.

To be lodged with Keeper of Records.

1. At any time after the filing of the originating statement, and not later than one month from the first conditional sanction of an advance, the vendor or his solicitor shall lodge with the Keeper of Records an abstract of the vendor's title, together with the original deeds and other muniments of title not theretofore lodged in Court. If the original of any document be not procurable, a copy, or such other evidence of its contents as can be obtained shall be lodged, except in the case of an outstanding mortgage of which the vendor or his solicitor has no copy, and the original of which is available for inspection.

If the deeds are numerous a deed box shall be lodged of such size as may be directed by the Keeper of Records, and in all cases a schedule of the deeds lodged must accompany the abstract.

The Keeper of Records shall receipt the abstract and issue a certificate of its lodgment, which shall forthwith be lodged in the Examiners' Office.

Preparation and verification of.

2. The abstract shall include all lands comprised in the originating statement, and shall be fairly and legibly written in roundhand on small brief paper, and on one side only, and with proper and distinct margins for the several parts of the instruments abstracted, and shall be verified by the solicitor by whom the same shall have been prepared, by an affidavit in Form 12. Abstracts of title shall be prepared in accordance with the directions in that behalf in the Appendix hereto.

If land be registered, land certificate to be lodged in lieu of abstract of title.

3. If the title to the lands be registered under the Local Registration of Title (Ireland) Act, 1891, the land certificate with the *lis pendens* entered thereon shall be lodged in lieu of an abstract of title.

ORDER XI.

RULINGS ON TITLE, AND ASCERTAINMENT OF SUPERIOR INTERESTS.

Rulings on title.

1. The rulings on title and directions for searches when given shall be transmitted to the vendor or his solicitor, and any requisitions thereon must be discharged on personal attendance

before an Examiner, and the mode in which each requisition is discharged shall be entered on the rulings and in the title-book. No person, except an officer of the Commission, shall write upon the rulings.

2. The draft requisition for searches in the Registry of Deeds shall be in Form 13, and shall be lodged in the Examiners' Office for settlement within one week of the issue of the directions for searches unless such directions necessitate the production of further evidence. The requisition must be lodged in the Registry of Deeds within three days from the settlement of the draft.

3. If the lands, or any part thereof, be held by the vendor under fee-farm grant, or lease, the Examiner shall, when ruling the title, make such requisitions as may be necessary to ascertain the particulars of any superior interest that may affect the lands; and all persons in receipt of, or entitled to any rent, fees, duties, services, or royalties issuing out of, or to be rendered in respect of the lands, shall be bound to furnish to the vendor, or his solicitor, such evidence as may be necessary to enable him to comply with such requisitions; and such persons shall be entitled to their costs reasonably incurred in connection therewith, the same to be paid by the vendor, or out of the proceeds of the sale.

ORDER XII.

AGREEMENT FOR PURCHASE AND APPLICATION FOR AN ADVANCE.

1. Agreements between vendor and tenant for the sale and purchase of a holding, with application for an advance, shall be in Form 10, or such other form as the Land Commission may from time to time direct. All such agreements shall be on stout writing medium paper, and be endorsed with the record number, title of the matter, county, and tenant's name, and shall be signed by both vendor and tenant, or some person acting under a power of attorney on behalf of either of them, and shall be verified by the affidavit of the tenant, and bear an Inland Revenue stamp or stamps to the value of sixpence, which must be cancelled according to law. Agreements shall be prepared in accordance with the directions in that behalf annexed to the form.

2. When the Agreement is signed by a person acting under power of attorney, the power of attorney or, if the original is enrolled in the High Court, a certified copy thereof shall be lodged and submitted to the Examiner to certify whether it is sufficient.

3. No Agreement shall be received after the expiration of one month from the date of the execution thereof by the tenant, unless it has to be executed by a person residing out of the United Kingdom, in which case it must be lodged within two months of the execution thereof by such person.

Agreement to be lodged within one month.

4. When two or more agreements for purchase in any one estate are lodged at the same time, they shall be accompanied by a summary by way of schedule in such form as the Land Commission may from time to time direct.

Schedule to be lodged with agreements.

5. No agreement for purchase shall be received which is not accurately filled up in accordance with the rules and directions, or which does not correspond with the schedule of areas furnished with the map.

Agreement not to be received if it is accurately prepared.

ORDER XIII.

MAPS AND SURVEYS.

1. Every agreement for purchase, subject as hereinafter mentioned, shall be accompanied by an Ordnance map, on the 6-inch scale, neatly mounted on strong linen, distinguishing thereon the exterior boundaries of the holding or holdings, and by such evidence of area as is hereinafter provided. Where the holdings are so small that the 6-inch scale is insufficient, an Ordnance map on the 25·344-inch scale may be used, or an enlargement of the smaller holdings may be made.

Map to be lodged with Agreement for purchase.

2. Maps shall be prepared and furnished by townlands, or groups of townlands; and should, when practicable, not exceed 18 inches by 12 inches in size, and in every case the names of the adjoining townlands should be shown upon the map. In no case should different maps be used for sales of different holdings upon the same townland.

Number and size of.

3. The maps must be accompanied by a certificate of the tenement valuation, and by a schedule of areas giving the contents of each separate plot and the total area of each holding, and shall be in the form used by the Ordnance Survey Department or such other form as the Land Commission may from time to time direct.

Certificate of valuation and schedule of areas.

4. If, for the purposes of proceedings in the Landed Estates Court, or Land Judges' Court, a survey of the estate has been made by the Ordnance Survey Department, the rental map shall be used if suitable. With the rental map shall be lodged a copy of the rental (if procurable), and a copy of the Ordnance Surveyor's report,

Landed Estate or Land Judges' Court rental map to be used if suitable.

accompanied by an affidavit from the vendor, his agent, or a competent surveyor in the employment of the vendor, stating that the several holdings are correctly marked on the map as they then exist, and the affidavit must state that the deponent visited the lands and examined the map upon the grounds.

5. If there has been no such survey as aforesaid, or, if the rental map be unsuitable, the latest revised Ordnance sheet, having the holdings marked thereon at the General Valuation Office, and verified in like manner, may be used.

Ordnance sheet marked at General Valuation Office may be used.

6. When trifling alterations have to be made in rental maps, or maps marked at the General Valuation Office, they shall be neatly made in a distinctive colour by a competent surveyor, who shall amend the areas as shown in the Ordnance Surveyor's report, or schedule of areas, and verify the same by an affidavit in which he shall state his qualification.

Alterations in map to be made and verified by surveyor.

7. Existing estate maps where suitable, and provided they are accompanied by proper evidence of area, and correspond with the Ordnance Survey as to names and townland boundaries, may be accepted at the discretion of the proper officer.

Estate maps may be used if suitable.

8. If the General Valuation Office map be very inaccurate or otherwise unsuitable, and if existing estate maps be not adopted, an Ordnance map with the holdings correctly delineated thereon, and accompanied by a schedule of areas, and certified by a competent surveyor, who shall state his qualifications, may be lodged; but where surveys of estates are necessary, they shall be made by the Ordnance Survey Department.

Surveys.

9. Directions for surveys by the Ordnance Survey Department may be obtained in the Agreements for Purchase Office, and the solicitor applying shall prepare such direction in Form 14, and shall furnish with it an ordnance sheet, showing the lands to be surveyed, and a certificate of the tenement valuation. With respect to surveys or revisions of surveys made by the Ordnance Survey Department, or maps or copies of maps and other documents drawn by or obtained from that department, the account shall be paid by the person at whose instance the work was done, or his solicitor, before the maps are delivered, or at each other period as that department shall direct. Every solicitor shall be personally responsible for the costs of any such survey made in pursuance of a direction issued at his instance.

Orders for survey; payment of account; liability of solicitor.

B 3

ORDER XIV.

INSPECTION OF HOLDING

Reference to Inspector. 1. Agreements for purchase and applications for advances shall be referred to an Inspector (being the Resident Inspector or one of the Assistant Commissioners), to report as to the security for the advance and such other matters as the Land Commission may direct, and in such form as they may from time to time direct.

Copies of report may be obtained. 2. The parties to the agreement or application may obtain certified copies of such report on payment of the prescribed fees.

Inspector to notify date of inspection to parties. 3. Due notification of the intention to inspect a holding shall be given by the Inspector to the parties to the agreement or application.

Inspector to ascertain boundaries, and certify map. 4. Upon the inspection the boundaries of the holding shall be ascertained by the Inspector, and the map, with such alterations if any as he shall find necessary, shall be certified by him to be correct.

ORDER XV.

CONDITIONAL SANCTION OF ADVANCE OR AGREEMENT FOR PURCHASE; NOTIFICATION TO PARTIES

Decision on application to be by order endorsed thereon. 1. The decision of the Commissioner on an application for an advance, or that an agreement for purchase shall be carried into effect by vesting order, shall be signified by a minute or order endorsed upon the agreement or application, and signed by the Commissioner.

Holding in two counties. 2. When a holding is situated in more counties than one the Commissioner, having regard to the area and value of the holding, shall determine and state in the order conditionally sanctioning the advance in which county such holding shall be deemed to be for the purposes of the Purchase of Land (Ireland) Act, 1891.

Advance not to be sanctioned until services and publications are vouched. 3. Except in the case of sales by the Land Judges or by the Land Commission, no advance shall be conditionally sanctioned until the services of the notice of filing of the originating statement, and the publication of the general notice to claimants have been vouched in the Registrar's Office, and a certificate to that effect has been endorsed upon the originating statement by the proper officer.

4. There shall be kept in the Agreements for Purchase Office a register of the persons directed to have notice of the filing of the originating statement, or who have entered appearances in the matter requiring notice of the sanction of sales, and their postal addresses, or those of their solicitors, and such persons or their solicitors may change the addresses from time to time, or have the register otherwise corrected ; provided every address so registered shall be one within the United Kingdom. Notice of the conditional sanction of every sale shall be transmitted through the post to the vendor and purchaser and all persons whose names appear on the register, or to the respective solicitors of such of the aforesaid persons as may be represented by solicitors : and any person whose rights may be prejudiced by the sale may within fourteen days of the date of such notice apply to the Commissioner upon notice to the other persons interested to vary or discharge his order.

Conditional sanction to be notified to persons interested.

5. If in the course of the investigation of the title, or otherwise in the course of the proceedings, a superior interest or incumbrance not disclosed in the originating statement is found to affect the lands, it shall be the duty of the Examiner to take the directions of the Commissioner as to the service of notice of the filing of the originating statement and of the sanction of such sales as may have been conditionally sanctioned upon the persons entitled to such superior interest or incumbrance, and no advance shall be conditionally sanctioned, nor shall any sale be completed until the services of such notices as may be directed have been vouched.

Notice to owners of superior interests and incumbrances not disclosed in originating statement.

6. When the Examiner ascertains that the claim of any person whose name is registered as entitled to notice of the sanction of sales has been discharged, he shall direct the name of such person to be struck out of the register.

Persons whose claim has been discharged not to receive further notifications.

ORDER XVI

VESTING ORDER.

1. As soon as the requisitions on title or other requirements preliminary to the making of a vesting order have been complied with, the Examiner shall either cause a draft of the vesting order to be prepared, or shall, if the Commissioner, with the assent of the Judicial Commissioner, permits a vesting order to be dispensed with, endorse upon the agreement for purchase a certificate to the effect that the same may be fiated by the Commissioner, specifying in such certificate the conditions, exceptions, and modifications (if any) subject to which the agreement may be so fiated.

When requisitions on title are discharged, Examiner to cause draft vesting order to be prepared, or certify that agreement may be fiated.

Draft vesting order to be settled by Examiner and approved by Commissioner.

2. All draft vesting orders shall be settled by the Examiner and submitted to the Commissioner for approval.

Examiner may direct two or more holdings to be vested by one order.

3. When two or more vesting orders on the same estate would, if made separately, be in a common or partly common form, the Examiner may direct that either the whole, or any portion of the estate shall be vested in the several purchasers by a single order.

Maps on vesting orders.

4. No map shall be endorsed upon, or referred to, in a vesting order unless a map of the lands being vested has been prepared for the purpose of proceedings in the Landed Estates Court, Ireland, or the Land Judges' Court, and is attached to a conveyance, order, or rental in such proceedings; in which case a copy of such map may be endorsed on the vesting order by the Ordnance Survey Department, and shall be referred to in such vesting order, and shall be sealed therewith.

Amount of stamp duty to be lodged.

5. The purchaser, or if the price of the land sold be inclusive of all expenses incidental to the purchase, the vendor or other the person having carriage of the proceedings, or their respective solicitors shall, when so directed by the Examiner, either have the purchaser's vesting order stamped, or lodge in Court the amount of the stamp duty payable thereon, or on the fiat in lieu thereof. The Examiner or an officer of his department shall assess the amount of the duty to be lodged in Court, and issue the necessary authority to enable its lodgment.

Execution of vesting order, or signing of fiat.

6. Vesting orders and fiats, when examined and certified by the Examiner, shall be presented to the Commissioner for execution, and in every case shall, unless already stamped, be accompanied by a receipt for the lodgment of the stamp duty payable thereon.

Stamping of vesting order or fiat.

7. The vesting orders when executed, or the agreements for purchase when fiated, shall, unless already stamped, be delivered by an officer of the Land Commission to the proper officer of the Inland Revenue for stamping.

Copy of vesting order to be filed.

8. A copy of every vesting order shall be filed in the Land Commission.

Rectification of vesting order.

9. An application to have a vesting order, or fiat in lieu thereof, corrected or rectified shall be by motion to a Judicial Commissioner; and a minute of the order for rectification when made shall be endorsed on the vesting order, or agreement for purchase, as the case may be, and signed by the Registrar.

ORDER XVII.

PROOF OF OCCUPANCY.

1. No vesting order or fiat in lieu thereof shall be executed, nor shall any advance to a purchaser be made, unless the Examiner be satisfied that the purchaser was alive, and, if he be tenant of the lands purchased, that he was in occupation of such lands within fourteen days of the date of the vesting order, fiat, or advance, as the case may be.

Examiner to to be satisfied as to occupancy of purchaser before execution of vesting order or fiat.

2. The vendor or other the person having carriage of the proceedings, or their respective solicitors, shall when required produce to the Examiner an affidavit, sworn not more than three days previously, verifying the occupancy of such of the purchasing tenants on the estate as are in occupation of their respective holdings, and to whom advances are about to be made, or whose vesting orders are about to be executed, or agreements about to be fiated. Such affidavit shall be in Form 13, and shall be made by the vendor, his agent, or some person who from local knowledge is capable of deposing to the facts therein stated.

Affidavit of occupancy.

ORDER XVIII.

MAKING OF ADVANCE AND CHARGING ORDER.

1. No advance shall be made to any purchaser who is fourteen days in arrear in the payment of any portion of the interest on his purchase money which has become payable.

Advance not to be made if interest in fourteen days in arrear.

2. An advance which does not exceed three-fourths of the price to be paid for the holding shall not be made until the purchaser shall have lodged in Court the balance of such price when such balance is payable in cash.

If advance does not exceed three-fourths of price, balance to be lodged in Court.

3. The final order for the making of an advance shall be prepared and certified by the Examiner, and shall, if the nature of the proceedings allow, bear even date with the vesting order or fiat as the case may be, and be presented to the Commissioner for signature therewith.

Final order for advance.

Charging order. 4. The vesting order shall, when practicable, charge the holding with the repayment of the advance. If a separate charging order be necessary, it shall be prepared by the Examiner, and shall be signed by the Commissioner, and sealed with the seal of the Land Commission.

ORDER XIX.

REGISTRATION OF PURCHASER'S OWNERSHIP.

Particulars to be transmitted to Registrar of Titles.

1. The particulars as to the holding to be prepared and transmitted by the Land Commission to the Registrar of Titles, in order that the title of the purchaser to the ownership of the holding may be registered pursuant to the Local Registration of Title (Ireland) Act, 1891, shall be as follows :—

(a.) The record number (if any) and title of the matter in which the purchase was made.

(b.) The date of the vesting order or fiat as the case may be.

(c.) The name, postal address, and occupation or other description of the purchaser.

(d.) The townland or townlands with the area in statute measure of the portion of each comprised in the holding, and the county and barony, and, if necessary for the purpose of identification, the parish in which each townland is situated.

(e.) The tenure of the purchaser at the date of the purchase as stated in the agreement for purchase, or ascertained by the Land Commission.

(f.) The particulars of the annuity payable in respect of the advance (if any) made by the Land Commission for the purchase of the holding.

(g.) The particulars of any other rentcharge reserved in the vesting order.

(h.) The particulars of any exceptions or reservations or superior interests subject to which the vesting order or fiat is made.

(j.) The particulars of any easement, right or appurtenance which the vesting order may declare the sale to be subject to or freed from.

(k.) Any other matter which the Examiner may consider necessary for the purposes of registration.

The particulars to be in a schedule.

2. Such particulars shall be embodied in a schedule which shall be prepared and certified by the Examiner, and signed by the Commissioner immediately after the execution of the vesting orders or the fiating of the agreements for purchase as the case may be. Each Examiner shall, if practicable, include in a single schedule the particulars of all holdings comprised in

the vesting orders, or agreements for sale, which he may present to the Commissioner for execution, or fiat on any one day; provided that if two or more holdings be vested by a single order a separate schedule may be used as regards the holdings comprised in such order.

3. The schedule shall be accompanied by an Ordnance sheet having the several holdings delineated thereon as they appear on the map used for the proceedings unless there be a map endorsed upon and referred to in the vesting orders, in which case a copy of such map may be endorsed upon the schedule by the Ordnance Survey Department, or the vesting orders may be produced to the Registrar of Titles for inspection. *Schedule to be accompanied by map.*

4. The schedule shall be lodged in the office of the Registrar of Titles by an officer of the Land Commission. *Schedule to be delivered to Registrar of Titles.*

ORDER XX.

APPORTIONMENT AND REDEMPTION OF SUPERIOR INTERESTS.

I. *Apportionment.*

1. Applications for the apportionment of tithe-rentcharge payable to the Land Commission, and of fixed annual instalments payable in lieu thereof, shall be made in Forms 16 and 17, and shall be lodged with the Superintendent of the Church Property Department of the Land Commission. *Apportionment of tithe-rentcharge and instalments in lieu thereof payable to the Commission.*

2. Applications for the apportionment of land improvement, or drainage charges payable to the Commissioners of Public Works in Ireland shall be made to such Commissioners, and the Examiner shall, if necessary, issue a requisition for that purpose. It shall be the duty of the vendor or his solicitor to furnish such evidence and documents as may be required for the apportionment. *Apportionment of land improvement and drainage charges.*

3. Applications for the apportionment of impropriate tithe-rentcharges, quit or crown rents, rents, fees, duties, services, rentcharges, or annuities, shall be made by motion on notice grounded upon a statement of facts. *Applications for apportionment of other superior interests to be grounded on statement of facts.*

4. The statement of facts shall be verified by the vendor, or his solicitor, or by such other person acquainted with the facts as the Commissioner may direct, and shall be fairly written on post paper, with sufficient margin, and filed in the Registrar's Office. If the superior interest to be apportioned be contributed by the owners of the lands subject thereto in certain proportions, and it is proposed to apportion in like manner, the particulars of the origin of such contribution, whether under a partition or otherwise, should be set forth in the statement. *Preparation and lodgment of statement of facts.*

The statement shall be accompanied by and refer to an ordnance map, showing the entire lands out of which the superior interest to be apportioned is payable, and the portions between which it is proposed to apportion the same, and shall also be accompanied by a certificate of the tenement valuation.

The map used for the purposes of the sale should be adopted when suitable; but the Commissioner may dispense with a map where it does not appear to him to be required.

Final order not to issue till sale completed. Draft to be furnished if required. 5. No final order for apportionment shall issue until the sale, or, if there be more sales than one, until one of the sales under the Land Purchase Acts which necessitated the apportionment has been completed either by the payment of the purchase money into Court, or by the execution of the vesting order, or fiating of the agreement for purchase. The person at whose instance such order is made shall, if required, furnish a draft of such order and the same shall be settled by the Registrar.

Sealed counterparts of apportionment order to be served to parties interested; printing of and maps thereon. 6. When a final order for apportionment has been made a sealed counterpart thereof, written or printed on stout hand-made paper or parchment, shall, except as hereinafter provided, be issued at the expense of the estate to the owner of the superior interest, and to the owner of any land upon which any portion of the superior interest which it is not intended to redeem has been apportioned. If four or more of such counterparts be required, the apportionment order shall be printed in such manner as the Land Commission may direct, and the original shall be filed in the Registrar's Office. If a map be referred to in the order it shall be drawn thereon by the Ordnance Survey Department. In the case of a quit or crown rent no such counterpart shall issue at the expense of the estate without the direction of the Commissioner.

Memorandum of apportionment to be endorsed on instrument creating superior interest. 7. A memorandum of the apportionment shall be endorsed by the Registrar upon the instrument creating the superior interest apportioned if such instrument be forthcoming.

Forms of statements of facts. 8. Statements of facts for the apportionment of impropriate tithe-rentcharges shall follow Form 18; for the apportionment of quit or crown rents shall follow Form 19; for the apportionment of rents, fees, duties, or services shall follow Form 20; and for the apportionment of rentcharges or annuities shall follow Form 21, with such variations and additions in each case as the circumstances may require.

Certificate and copy of statement to be lodged when application is for apportionment of impropriate tithe-rentcharge, or quit or crown rent. 9. When application is made for the apportionment of an impropriate tithe-rentcharge, or of a quit or crown rent, the tithe-rentcharge or quit rent certificate, as the case may be, and a copy of the statement of facts shall be lodged with the original, and the Registrar shall transmit such copy to the Superintendent of the Church Property Department of the Land Commission, or to the Quit Rent Office, as the case may be, for report; and no application for apportionment shall be moved without the leave of the Commissioner until such report has been obtained.

10. When application is made for the apportionment of any rent, fees, duties or services, or of a rentcharge or annuity, the instrument creating the superior interest to be apportioned shall be furnished with the statement of facts, unless it be already lodged in Court.

II. Redemption.

11. When any quit or crown rent, or land improvement or drainage charge, is being redeemed, the vendor or his solicitor shall produce to the Examiner at the vouching of the allocation schedule, a receivable order from the Quit Rent Office, or the Board of Public Works, as the case may be, to enable the redemption money and arrears, if any, to be lodged to the proper account in the Bank of Ireland. Such receivable order shall specify separately the amount of the redemption money and of the arrears, and shall allow at least seven clear days from the date of vouching for lodgment. When tithe rentcharge payable to the Land Commission or fixed annual instalments payable in lieu thereof are being redeemed, the vendor or his solicitor shall produce at such vouching a memorandum from the Church Property Department of the amount required for the redemption thereof, and of the arrears thereof.

12. The application for an order for the redemption of any other superior interest, or of any apportioned part thereof shall, if made by the person entitled thereto, be made on notice to the vendor, and if made by the vendor shall be made on notice to the reputed owner of such superior interest. Service must also be made on such other persons as may have entered appearances requiring notice of such an application, or as would appear to be affected by such redemption.

13. When the redemption of any such superior interest as in the last preceding Rule mentioned (other than impropriate tithe rentcharge) or of any apportioned part thereof shall have been ordered, unless the price be agreed upon between the parties, or the determining of it referred to the Land Commission, within fourteen days from the date of the order, or within such further period as the Commissioner shall direct, the person who applied for such order shall serve upon the other party a request in writing to appoint an arbitrator following Form 22.

14. The submission to an Arbitration Court and the appointment of the arbitrator or arbitrators and umpire shall be in Form 23, or in accordance therewith, and shall be fairly written upon foolscap paper, with sufficient margin, and be lodged in the Registrar's Office before the first sitting of the Arbitration Court. It shall be the duty of the officer receiving such submission to arbitration to see that the signatures thereto are proved by affidavit.

Award

15. The award shall be on foolscap paper, with sufficient margin, and shall follow Form 24, as nearly as the circumstances of the case admit, and shall determine who is to bear the costs of the arbitration. When either party desires the award of a Court of Arbitration to be recorded, he shall within ten days from the making of such award serve notice on the opposite party of his intention to apply to the Court for such purpose. As soon as the Court orders the award to be recorded it shall be filed in the Registrar's Office together with the submission.

Vouching of title to superior interest.

16. The person entitled to the price or compensation payable in respect of a superior interest, or his solicitor, shall, unless there be a sufficient reason to the contrary, attend before the Examiner on the vouching of the allocation schedule to prove his claim, and for that purpose shall, unless his title has already been investigated, file an affidavit which shall be prepared in accordance with the directions in the Appendix hereto, and such affidavit may be lodged with the Examiner at any time after the redemption of the superior interest has been ordered.

Price of superior interest may be placed to a private credit and invested.

17. If by reason of incumbrances affecting a superior interest or for any other reason the price or compensation payable in respect thereof cannot be distributed at the general allocation, the Commissioner may order such price or compensation to be paid into the Bank of Ireland to such credit as he may direct, and may make such order as may be just as to the investment thereof, and as to the payment of the dividends and interest thereon pending its distribution.

Memorandum of redemption of superior interest to be endorsed on instrument creating same.

18. Except in the case of quit or crown rents, tithe-rentcharges, and land improvement or drainage charges, a memorandum of the redemption of a superior interest or of any apportioned part thereof shall be endorsed by the Registrar upon the instrument creating such superior interest, unless such instrument be retained in Court.

ORDER XXI.

ALLOCATION.

I.—*Proceeds of sales by vendors to tenants not paid into the High Court.*

Vendor to prepare allocation schedule.

1. As soon as an advance shall have been made, unless such advance has been paid into the High Court, the vendor or his solicitor shall prepare an allocation schedule in Form 25.

2. The allocation schedule shall be vouched before the Examiner, and the case shall be then listed by him for allocation by the Commissioner.

II.—*Interest on purchase money collected by the Land Commission.*

3. Applications for the payment of interest on purchase money, accruing between the date of the agreement for purchase and the date upon which the advance is made by any person other than the person in receipt of the rents at the date of the agreement for purchase, shall be made to the Commissioner by motion on notice.

III.—*Proceeds of the sale of a holding sold by the Land Commission.*

4. All moneys received in respect of the proceeds of the sale by the Land Commission of a holding which was subject to an annuity payable to them shall be lodged to a credit to be entitled "In the matter of Section 38 of the Land Law (Ireland) Act, 1896, and of the proceeds of the sale of the holding of [*here name the proprietor who obtained the advance from the Land Commission*] in the lands of   , Barony   , County   ;" and the Examiner shall issue a privity or receivable order to enable such lodgment to be made. Moneys so lodged shall not be allocated except in pursuance of an order signed by a Commissioner.

5. All notices, affidavits, consents and orders in reference to the allocation shall be headed "Court of the Irish Land Commission" and be entitled as in Rule 4 of this Order.

6. It shall be the duty of the Solicitor to the Land Commission to obtain as soon as possible from the Commissioner an order for the payment of all moneys due to the Land Commission in respect of the holding, and of all expenses incurred by the Land Commission in relation to the sale or otherwise with respect to the holding, and if there be any surplus after such payments he shall fill up and transmit to the Examiners' Office a form specifying the date of the sale, the amount realized, the particulars of the payments made, the amount of the surplus, the date on which the advance was made to the purchasing tenant of the holding, the name of such tenant, the amount of the advance, and the full title of the matter in which such advance was made; and all subsequent directions and rulings in reference to the

matter shall, so far as possible, be written on such form. The Examiner shall thereupon send for the land certificate evidencing the title of the proprietor whose holding had been sold, and if it shall appear therefrom that the title to the tenancy prior to the purchase by the tenant had been investigated, the Examiner shall report as to who appears to him to be entitled to the surplus.

Examiner to give directions.

7. If such title has not been investigated, the Examiner shall send for the agreement for sale to the purchasing tenant, the lease (if any), and any other document in the custody of the Land Commission which would help to disclose the title of the tenant prior to his purchase, and he shall note the nature of the tenancy, the date at which according to the agreement for purchase the tenant became entitled, the incumbrances (if any) disclosed in the agreement for purchase, and any information as to the title of the former proprietor disclosed by the title books, collection books, or otherwise, and he shall give such directions for the guidance of the Solicitor to the Land Commission as he shall think fit in reference to communications to be addressed to the former proprietor, to incumbrancers, or to other persons appearing to be interested in such surplus.

Correspondence to be dealt with by Solicitor to Commission.

8. All correspondence in reference to the allocation shall be referred to and dealt with by the Solicitor to the Land Commission, subject to any directions given by the Commissioner or Examiner.

Application for payment : searches.

9. All applications for payment shall, together with any accompanying evidence, be laid before the Examiner, who shall thereupon make such requisitions as he may think necessary. It shall not be necessary to require any search other than a common search against the lands, and if title is being shown to a yearly tenancy such search shall not commence prior to the 1st January, 1870, or the date of the creation of the tenancy if of a later date. If the amount involved be £50 or under, a hand search will be sufficient.

Discharge of requisitions.

10. If the applicant be represented by a solicitor, a copy of the Examiner's rulings shall be transmitted to such solicitor, and he shall be at liberty to write his replies opposite to the requisitions, but the requisitions are to be discharged by the Examiner upon the original rulings. If the applicant be not so represented and the amount involved be £50 or under, it shall be the duty of the Solicitor to the Land Commission to make the necessary searches, and, so far as possible, to comply with the requisitions of the Examiner, and any costs necessarily incurred by him shall be defrayed out of the fund.

11. The Examiner shall, as soon as his requisitions shall have been complied with, make his report at the foot of his rulings as to the person or persons appearing to him to be entitled to receive payment of the fund, and such report shall be laid before the Commissioner, who shall proceed to make his order thereon. The report shall then be filed in the Registrar's Office.

Report and payment.

IV.—*General.*

12. Upon every application for payment a certificate of funds signed by the Accountant must be produced.

Certificate of funds to be produced on application for payment.

ORDER XXII.

INVESTMENTS.

1. The stockbrokers for the time being appointed by the Lord Chancellor to carry out the investment of funds under the control of the Supreme Court of Judicature in Ireland shall be stockbrokers to the Land Commission; and such stockbrokers shall discharge their duties in such order or rotation or otherwise as the Land Commission may from time to time direct.

Stockbrokers of Supreme Court to act for Land Commission.

2. Whenever an order shall be made for the purchase of stock or securities with money standing to the account of the Land Commission, the price shall not be paid to the broker until he shall have transferred to the account of the Land Commission stock or securities equal in value to the money to be invested, deducting his commission; and whenever an order shall be made for the sale of stock or securities standing to the account of the Land Commission, the same shall not be transferred until the broker shall have lodged in the Bank of Ireland to the account of the Land Commission the price thereof, deducting his commission.

Payment of price and transfer of stock.

ORDER XXIII.

GUARANTEE DEPOSITS.

1. Guarantee deposits shall be made of pounds only.

To be in pounds only.

2. No guarantee deposit in cash shall be received unless accompanied by a privity in Form 26. Application for such privity shall be made by the party lodging the guarantee deposit, or his solicitor, and the privity shall be signed by the Examiner, and transmitted to the Accountant.

Privity for lodgment of.

3. A register shall be kept in the Accountant's office of all guarantee deposits, stating the names of the persons entitled to or interested in them, the names of the persons entitled to receive the interest thereon, and the lands to which they apply, and the securities (if any) in which they are invested.

Register of.

Registration of guarantee deposits lodged in cash. 4. When a guarantee deposit is lodged in cash, the Accountant shall register it in the name of the person whose name appears in the privity, and the interest shall be payable to him from the date of the advance.

Registration in other cases. 5. In all cases not otherwise provided for, the guarantee deposits shall be registered in the title of the matter until a Land Judge or the Commissioner, as the case may be, shall declare in whose name they are to be registered, and to whom the interest shall be paid, and such declaration, if made by the Commissioner, shall where practicable be made when the funds are being allocated.

Registrar to draw up direction as to registration. 6. When a Land Judge makes a declaratory order concerning the registration of guarantee deposits, or the payment of the interest thereon, the Registrar of the Land Commission shall draw up a direction in accordance with such order and transmit the same to the Accountant; and for that purpose it shall be the duty of the person at whose instance the order shall have been made, or of his solicitor, to furnish to the Registrar such documents as may be required.

Certificate of entry on register of. 7. The Accountant may upon the application of any person entered upon the register as entitled to or interested in a guarantee deposit, or of his solicitor, or, by leave of the Commissioner, upon the application of any other person, issue to such person a certificate of the entry on the register.

Transmission of interest in. 8. Any person becoming entitled to or interested in any guarantee deposit may apply to the Commissioner for a ruling to have his rights as regards such guarantee deposit entered upon the register, and the Accountant shall enter a minute of such ruling on the register.

Investment of. 9. Applications for the investment of guarantee deposits shall be made on notice to all parties interested therein. All such investments shall be made in the name of the Land Commission, and the expenses of and incident to such investments shall be paid or provided by the applicant.

Certificate of entry on register to be produced on all applications. 10. Upon all applications concerning guarantee deposits standing to the credit of matters, the certificate of the entry on the register of guarantee deposits shall be produced.

Payment of interest on. 11. The dividends on the guaranteed land stock retained for guarantee deposits and the interest or dividends on guarantee deposits otherwise invested, shall be payable immediately after the respective dates upon which the Land Commission shall receive such interest or dividends, and shall on the occasion of the first payment after investment be calculated from the date of such investment. There shall be deducted from the first payment of dividend after investment (if not otherwise provided) the expenses of and incident to the investment, and the proportion of dividend which accrued up to the date of the investment. The proportion of dividend so deducted may be either retained by the Land Commission as uninvested guarantee deposits, or invested in the same securities at their discretion.

12. Applications for payment to the persons entitled thereto of guarantee deposits retained in respect of advances under the Purchase of Land (Ireland) Act, 1891, or the Redemption of Rent (Ireland) Act, 1891, shall be made by letter addressed to the Secretary of the Land Commission. The application shall be referred to the Accountant, and if he certifies that no part of the guarantee deposit has been actually applied towards the payment of a debt declared to be irrecoverable, it shall be laid before the Commissioner for consideration and direction.

Applications for payment of guarantee deposits in respect of sales under Acts of 1891 to be by letter.

13. The Accountant shall, as regards each estate, report from time to time to the Commissioner how much of the advances, made otherwise than under the Purchase of Land (Ireland) Act, 1891, or the Redemption of Rent (Ireland) Act, 1891, and in respect of which guarantee deposits have been provided, are ascertained to have been repaid at the end of each decade of the annuity, and the particulars of the entry on the register as regards such guarantee deposits. The Commissioner may thereupon make such order as may be necessary for the payment out of such guarantee deposits of a sum equal to the portion of the advance so ascertained to have been repaid.

Payment out of proportion of guarantee deposits in respect of other sales.

14. When there has been repaid on account of any advance a sum equal to the guarantee deposit, the Accountant shall report the fact to the Commissioner, together with the particulars of the entry on the register. The Commissioner may thereupon make such order as may be necessary for the payment of the guarantee deposit, or any outstanding balance thereof.

Payment of guarantee deposits generally.

15. If for any reason any sum payable in respect of a guarantee deposit under Rules 13 and 14 of this Order cannot be immediately paid to the person or persons entitled thereto, the Commissioner may order such sum to be paid to such credit as he may direct, and may make such order as may be just as to the investment thereof, and as to the payment of the dividends or interest thereon pending its payment out of Court to the person or persons entitled thereto.

Guarantee deposit may be placed to separate credit and invested.

ORDER XXIV.

PAYMENT INTO BANK OF IRELAND UNDER SECTION 14 OF THE LAND LAW (IRELAND) ACT, 1887.

1. Before making any application under sec. 14, sub-sec. 1 of the Land Law (Ireland) Act, 1887, for payment of advances into the Bank of Ireland, the applicant or his solicitor shall attend before the Examiner with the documents and other evidence upon which such application is grounded.

Applicant to attend before Examiner.

2. The Examiner shall thereupon ascertain that all necessary preliminaries to the making of the advances have been complied with, and that the holdings could forthwith be vested in the purchasers, or the agreements for purchase fiated, and he shall issue a certificate or report to that effect, and shall state therein

Report of Examiner.

34

if he has any reason to believe that the parties are not entitled *prima facie* to carry out the agreements for sale, and any other matter which should be brought under the notice of the Commissioner.

Application to Commissioner.

3. The application to the Commissioner shall then be made on notice to all persons who have entered general appearances or appearances requiring notice of such an application, and such other persons as the Examiner may direct, and shall be grounded upon the report of the Examiner, the originating statement, the rulings on title, if issued, and any other evidence tending to show the nature and particulars of the vendor's estate in the lands, and the charges affecting the same.

No order to be made until vesting orders or date are ready for execution.

4. An order for payment into the Bank of Ireland shall not be made unless the vesting orders are ready for execution, or the agreements for purchase are ready to be dated.

ORDER XXV.

APPOINTMENT OF TRUSTEES.

I.—*Trustees for the purposes of the Settled Land Acts, 1882 to 1890.*

To be by motion on notice.

1. Applications for the appointment of trustees for the purposes of the Settled Land Acts, 1882 to 1890, shall be made by motion on notice as in Form 27, with such modifications as the circumstances of the case may require.

Procedure to be otherwise, as in Chancery Division.

2. The procedure shall otherwise be in accordance with the General Rules and Orders and practice for the time being regulating the procedure in similar applications to the Chancery Division of the High Court, in so far as such rules, orders, and practice may be applicable.

II.—*Appointment under Section 60 of the Landed Estates Court Act.*

Application to be by statement of facts.

3. Applications for the appointment of trustees under section 60 of the Landed Estates Court Act shall be made by statement of facts as in Form 28, with such modifications as the circumstances of the case may require. The statement shall be fairly written on post paper with sufficient margin, shall be verified by the affidavit of the applicant, or, if the Commissioner so permit, by the affidavit of his solicitor, and shall be filed in the Registrar's office.

Documents to be lodged therewith.

4. Together with the statement there shall be lodged a copy of the instrument creating the trusts, and any consents, or other documents necessary to support the application. The statement and other documents shall be laid before the Commissioner for his directions.

ORDER XXVI.

PARTITION AND EXCHANGE.

1. An application by either landlord or tenant for a partition, exchange, or division of land held by tenants in common, or rundale or intermixed plots, under sec. 11 of the Purchase of Land (Ireland) Act, 1885, shall be in writing on foolscap paper with proper margin, and shall be verified by the affidavit of the applicant, and be filed in the Registrar's Office. The application shall state:— *Application to be in writing.*

The names and addresses of the several tenants of the land so held in common or rundale or intermixed plots.

The Ordnance Survey name and gross acreage of such land, and the barony and county in which it is situate.

If the original letting was not a joint letting, when and how the holding came to be so held.

The terms of the original letting of such land by the landlord, and the amount of the gross yearly rent payable.

The names of the several tenants paying the said rent, and the proportions in which they pay it.

2. On the lodgment of any such application the Commissioner may appoint one or more surveyor or surveyors to inspect the lands, and divide the same into convenient and separate holdings, to apportion the gross rent payable out of the entire lands on such apportioned holdings, and to state the names of the tenants of such holdings, and the apportioned rents to be thenceforth payable by them. *Appointment of surveyor.*

3. The surveyor's report and scheme for partition shall be lodged in the Registrar's Office, and notice thereof shall be given to the landlord, the several tenants, and all such other persons as the Commissioner shall direct, in Form 29. *Lodgment of surveyor's report, notice thereof.*

4. If no application be made to the Commissioner within fourteen days from such notice, or within such further time as the Commissioner shall direct, to vary or amend the said report and scheme for partition, and if it shall appear expedient to the Commissioner, the same shall stand confirmed and a final order for partition shall be made in accordance with such report and scheme or in accordance with any order amending the same. *Confirmation of report.*

5. No final order for partition, exchange, or division shall issue until the sale which necessitated such partition, exchange, or division, as the case may be, shall have been completed. *Final order not to issue until sale completed.*

6. A draft of the order shall be prepared by the applicant, or his solicitor, and lodged with the Examiner for settlement. *Draft of order to be lodged with Examiner.*

7. The draft order, when settled by the Examiner, and approved by the Commissioner, shall be printed in such manner as the Land Commission may direct. The engrossment shall be sealed with the seal of the Land Commission, and then laid before the Commissioner for his signature. *Order to be printed, and signed by Commissioner.*

c 2

8. A counterpart of the order shall be issued to the landlord, and to each tenant entitled to a share of the lands.

ORDER XXVII.

SPECIFIC PERFORMANCE.

An application by a vendor or purchaser for a decree for specific performance shall be by motion on notice to the other party, and if such application be by the vendor, the notice of motion shall be served personally on the purchaser unless he be represented by a solicitor other than the vendor's solicitor, or unless the Commissioner shall otherwise direct.

ORDER XXVIII.

CHANGE OF PARTIES BY DEATH, &C.

1. A person claiming to be entitled to have the proceedings continued in his name by reason of the death of the vendor, or transmission or change of his interest, shall, before applying to the Commissioner, obtain a report from the Examiner upon his title to have the proceedings so continued in his name.

2. If a purchasing tenant becomes divested of his interest in his holding by death, bankruptcy, assignment, or otherwise, after the agreement for purchase has been executed, but before the holding has been vested, or such agreement fiated, the person claiming to be entitled to the purchasing tenant's interest in the holding, or a solicitor duly authorized on his behalf, shall attend before the Examiner to prove the title of such person, and that he is in occupation of the holding; and thereupon the Examiner may either himself take the direction of the Commissioner (such direction to be endorsed on the agreement for purchase) as to the person in whom the holding is to be vested, or he may direct a motion to be made on the subject.

ORDER XXIX.

PERSONS UNDER DISABILITY.

1. The order appointing any person to act as guardian or next friend of a person under disability, shall be served on such guardian or next friend, and all notices and orders subsequently served upon such persons, shall be deemed to have been duly served upon the party so under disability.

2. When any married woman, not entitled for her separate use, joins in or consents to any application to the Land Commission, the Commissioner shall before making an order be satisfied that such married woman is aware of the nature and effect of the application, and that she freely consents thereto, and for this purpose an appointment shall be made with the solicitor for her attendance before the Commissioner, for the purpose of being examined, or the Commissioner may, at his discretion, appoint some solicitor to make such examination, who shall for that purpose be furnished with a copy of the application; and the solicitor so appointed shall certify to the Commissioner that he has made such examination, and the result thereof, and his certificate shall be verified by affidavit. *Consent of married woman.*

ORDER XXX.

MOTIONS AND ORDERS.

I.—*Motions.*

1. Applications to a Commissioner shall be made to him in person or in such manner as each Commissioner shall from time to time prescribe. *Applications to a Commissioner.*

2. In the case of a motion on notice, a certificate of the appearances entered in the matter must be produced at the hearing of such motion. *Certificate of appearances to be produced at hearing.*

3. There shall be at least two clear days between the service of a notice of motion and the day on which the same is heard, and, if the notice be served outside the municipal boundary of the city of Dublin, there shall be at least four clear days. *What notice to be given.*

4. If the application be made *ex parte*, the applicant shall, before moving the Commissioner, lodge with the Registrar a docket stating the nature of the application, and referring to the documents, or other evidence, upon which the same is grounded. *Ex parte motions.*

5. The following applications when made shall be assigned to a Judicial Commissioner:— *Applications to be assigned to a Judicial Commissioner.*

(a.) In reference to requisitions on title made by an Examiner.

(b.) For appointment of trustees.

(c.) For a decree for specific performance.

(d.) In reference to the apportionment, redemption, or satisfaction of superior interests, other than applications for the payment of the redemption money of quit or crown rents, of rents or tithe-rentcharges payable to the Land Commission, or fixed annual instalments payable in lieu of tithe-rentcharge, or of land improvement or drainage charges.

(a) By an incumbrancer, an owner of a superior interest, or other person interested to vary or discharge an order conditionally sanctioning an advance or agreement for purchase as being prejudicial to the interests of the applicant.

(*f.*) To continue proceedings in the name of a person claiming by reason of the death of the vendor, or transmission or change of his interest, when the Examiner's report is against the granting of the application.

(*g.*) Motions made by direction of an Examiner in reference to the title to a holding when a purchasing tenant becomes divested of his interest therein before the completion of the purchase.

Provided always that with a view to the prompt hearing of any such application, the Judicial Commissioner may at any time direct that any of such applications shall be assigned to the Commissioner before whom the proceedings in the matter are pending, or to such other Commissioner as he may appoint.

Side-bar orders.

6. The following shall be side-bar orders :—

(*a.*) To make a conditional order (other than an order for attachment) absolute, when no cause has been shown, or the cause shown has been disallowed.

(*b.*) To allow cause shown and discharge conditional order when no motion has been made to disallow the cause.

(*c.*) For an order on any person to lodge deeds.

(*d.*) For a writ of sequestration for disobedience to an order of the Court.

(*e.*) For a writ of *fieri facias* to enforce payment of costs awarded by order.

(*f.*) For an order to the sheriff to put a purchaser from the Land Commission into possession of the lands purchased subject as is provided by Order XLVIII.

II.—*Orders*

Orders which may be entered on the allocation schedule.

7. Orders for payment or investment or for the sale of securities, or other rulings of the Commissioner in reference to the allocation of the fund may be entered on the allocation schedule.

Orders which may be entered in ruling book.

8. Orders which are in the nature of directions to an officer of the Court to do, or to omit to do any act, or to act upon, or reject evidence tendered, or directions to the person having carriage of the proceedings as to the conduct thereof, shall be entered in the ruling book.

All others to be entered in order book.

9. All other rulings and orders save such as are signed by a Commissioner, or such as are directed by rule to be printed, shall be entered in the order book.

To be signed by Registrar.

10. All orders shall, unless otherwise directed by rule, be signed by the Registrar.

Registrar shall, if required, prepare order in conformity with any ruling.

11. The Registrar shall, at the instance of any party interested, prepare an order in conformity with any ruling of a Commissioner entered upon the allocation schedule or ruling book.

ORDER XXXL

Cause against Conditional Order.

1. Any person desiring to show cause against a conditional order must enter an appearance, and serve on the vendor and the person on whose application such order was obtained, or their respective solicitors, a notice of cause referring to any affidavit or other document on which he relies.

2. Unless the person at whose instance such order was obtained, shall, within the time specified in the conditional order, or within four days thereafter, serve a notice of motion to make the same absolute, the person showing cause may have a rule entered in the Registrar's office allowing his cause; and on such rule being entered he may proceed to tax his costs of resisting such conditional order.

3. If no cause be shown within the time specified, or if the cause be disallowed, the solicitor for the person who obtained the order shall attend in the Registrar's office to prove the services of the conditional order, and that no cause has been shown, or that the cause has been disallowed, and thereupon the Registrar shall, except in the case of an order for attachment, proceed to make up the absolute order.

ORDER XXXII.

Evidence and Examination of Witnesses.

I. *Evidence generally.*

1. The evidence of witnesses shall, unless there be reason to the contrary, be by affidavit; but any witness may by leave of the Commissioner be examined orally before the Commissioner.

2. All writs, records, pleadings, affidavits, and other documents that might be read and received in evidence in the High Court, may be read and received in evidence in the Land Commission; and office copies of all such writs and other records and documents shall be admissible in evidence to the same extent as the originals would be.

II. *Examination of witnesses.*

3. The depositions of witnesses examined orally shall be taken down in writing by the Registrar or other officer of the Court, not ordinarily by question and answer, but so as to represent as nearly as may be the statement of the witness: provided that

the Commissioner may order any party who shall produce any witness or witnesses for examination, to provide a competent shorthand writer, who shall be paid in the first instance by such party, to take down the evidence of such witness or witnesses under the direction of the Commissioner, and for the use of the Court; and the Commissioner shall make such order as he may consider just as to the costs of providing such shorthand writer; and the transcript of the notes of such shorthand writer shall be lodged with the Registrar, and any party interested may have a copy of the same on payment of the sum of three halfpence for every seventy-two words.

Witness to be subject to cross-examination.
4. Any witness examined orally shall be subject to cross-examination and re-examination; and when any party to proceedings shall have filed an affidavit, whether made by himself, or by any witness, such party, or witness, shall be subject to cross-examination and re-examination, and shall be bound to attend for the purpose of being cross-examined, upon being served with notice to that effect two days before the time of such cross-examination if resident in Dublin or within ten miles thereof, or four days if resident elsewhere in Ireland, and upon tender to any such witness, other than the party himself, of his reasonable expenses; and such expenses shall be paid in the first instance by the person requiring such cross-examination.

Examination by commission.
5. Application to have a witness or witnesses examined by commission shall be made by motion on notice. The commission shall be in Form 30; shall be sealed with the seal of the Court, and signed by the Registrar; and shall issue on such terms or conditions as to costs or otherwise as the Commissioner may think fit; and the examination shall in all respects be subject to the regulations for the time being in force for the examination of witnesses by commissions issuing out of the High Court, as if the Land Commissioner were the Judge, and the Court of the Land Commission were the High Court.

III. *Summonses for attendance of witnesses.*

Form of.
6. Summonses for the attendance of witnesses, and for the production of documents before the Land Commission shall be in Form 81, and shall be signed by the Registrar.

Service of; expenses.
7. The service of a summons shall be effected by delivering a copy thereof, and at the same time producing the original. The reasonable travelling expenses of the witness must be tendered when the summons is being served.

Punishment for disobedience to.
8. Any person wilfully disobeying a summons, or order for his attendance for the purpose of being examined or producing any document, shall be deemed guilty of contempt of Court, and may be dealt with accordingly.

ORDER XXXIII.

AFFIDAVITS.

1. Affidavits, affirmations, or declarations sworn or made in Ireland, may be sworn or made before any person authorized to administer oaths for the purposes of the High Court, or before a Justice of the Peace for the county or borough in which the affidavit, affirmation, or declaration is sworn or made.

Before whom to be sworn in Ireland.

2. Affidavits, affirmations, or declarations may be sworn or made in England or Scotland, or the Channel Islands, or the Isle of Man, or in any colony, island, plantation, or place under the dominion of Her Majesty in foreign parts, before any Judge, Court, notary public, or person lawfully authorized to administer oaths in such country, colony, island, plantation, or place, respectively, or before any British ambassador, envoy, minister, chargé d'affaires, or secretary of embassy or legation, exercising his functions in any foreign country, or any British consul-general, consul, vice-consul, acting consul, pro-consul, or consular agent, exercising his functions in any foreign place in that country or place, and the Commissioners and other officers of the Land Commission shall take judicial notice of the seal or signature, as the case may be, of any of the aforesaid persons.

Before whom to be sworn out of Ireland.

3. Every affidavit shall be drawn up in the first person, and shall be divided into paragraphs, and every paragraph shall be numbered consecutively, and as nearly as may be shall be confined to a distinct portion of the subject. The affidavit shall state the description and true place of abode of the deponent, and also what facts or circumstances deposed to are within deponent's own knowledge, and his means of knowledge, and what facts or circumstances deposed to are known to or believed by him by reason of information derived from other sources than his own knowledge, and what such sources are.

Preparation.

4. The time and place of swearing the affidavit shall be stated in the jurat, and all persons authorized to take affidavits for the Land Commission, shall certify in the jurat of every affidavit taken by them that they know either the deponent himself or some person named in the jurat who certifies his knowledge of the deponent. When an affidavit is sworn by any person who appears to the officer taking the affidavit to be illiterate or blind, the officer shall certify in the jurat that the affidavit was read in his presence to the deponent, that the deponent seemed perfectly to understand it, and that the deponent made his signature in the presence of the officer. No such affidavit shall be used in evidence in the absence of this certificate, unless the Commissioner is otherwise satisfied that the affidavit was read over to and appeared to be perfectly understood by the deponent.

Jurat.

Alterations to be authenticated.

5. No affidavit having in the jurat or body thereof any interlineation, alteration, or erasure shall without leave of the Commissioner, be filed, read, or made use of in any matter, unless the interlineation or alteration (other than by erasure) is authenticated by the initials of the person taking the affidavit, nor in the case of an erasure, unless the words or figures appearing at the time of taking the affidavit to be written on the erasure are rewritten and signed or initialled in the margin of the affidavit by the person taking it.

Commissioner may receive notwithstanding irregularity.

6. The Commissioner may, on such terms as he may think fit, receive any affidavit notwithstanding any defect or irregularity in the form thereof or in the jurat, and may direct a memorandum to be made on the document that it has been so received.

Not to be sworn before the vendor or solicitor for party.

7. No affidavit shall be sufficient if sworn before the vendor in the matter, his agent, or solicitor, or if sworn before the solicitor for the person on whose behalf the affidavit is to be used.

Not to be sworn before clerk or agent, &c., of solicitor for party.

8. Any affidavit which would be insufficient if sworn before the solicitor for a party to the proceedings, shall be insufficient if sworn before such solicitor's partner or clerk, agent or correspondent, or the clerk or partner of such agent or correspondent.

ORDER XXXIV.

SEQUESTRATION AND ATTACHMENT.

Obedience to order may be enforced by attachment or sequestration.

1. The Commissioner may, to enforce obedience to any order, cause a writ of attachment or sequestration to issue against any party in default.

I.—Sequestration.

In the case of disobedience to an order, writ of sequestration may issue.

2. Where any person is by any order directed to pay money into Court, or to do any other act within a limited time, and, after due service of such order, refuses or neglects to obey the same according to the exigency thereof, the person prosecuting such order shall, at the expiration of the time limited for the performance thereof, be entitled, without obtaining any order for that purpose, to issue a writ of sequestration against the estate and effects of such disobedient person. Such writ shall have the same effect as a writ of sequestration in the Chancery Division of the High Court has heretofore had, and the proceeds of such sequestration may be dealt with in the same manner as the proceeds of writs of sequestration have heretofore been dealt with by the said Chancery Division.

Method of obtaining form of.

3. Any person entitled to issue a writ of sequestration under the preceding rule shall, before issuing the same, apply to the Registrar to approve of one or more sequestrators, and to obtain directions as to his or their security and accounting. On a

certificate from the Registrar of the approval of such person or persons the writ may issue directed to such person or persons in Form 32, and it shall be sealed with the seal of the Land Commission and signed by the Registrar.

4. One sequestrator only shall be named in the writ, unless the Commissioner shall otherwise direct. *One sequestrator shall be named.*

5. Every sequestrator shall enter into security by recognizance or otherwise, as the Commissioner shall direct, and the amount and nature of such security shall be directed, and the securities approved of by the Registrar, upon the application mentioned in Rule 8 of this Order, or by the Commissioner. A sequestrator shall not enter upon the execution of the writ until he has obtained a memorandum, signed by the Registrar, that he has duly perfected his security. *Sequestrator to give security.*

6. Every sequestrator shall be bound to account before the Registrar, as shall be directed upon his appointment, or at any time by the Commissioner, and not less than once in every year, unless the Commissioner shall otherwise direct. *Sequestrator to account.*

II.—Attachment.

7. No writ of attachment shall be issued without the leave of the Commissioner, to be applied for on notice to the party against whom the attachment is to be issued. *To be applied for on notice.*

8. Every writ of attachment and order of committal for contempt shall be headed "Court of the Irish Land Commission, Land Purchase Acts," and, if issued in consequence of disobedience to an order, shall be entitled in the matter in which such order was made. The writ of attachment or order of committal shall be directed to the sheriff of the county where the party to be attached or committed resides or is to be found, or to any peace officer, or to such other person as the Commissioner may direct, and shall be sealed with the seal of the Land Commission and signed by the Registrar. In the case of a committal order the order shall recite the particulars of the disobedience or other contempt occasioning its issue. *Form of attachment or committal.*

ORDER XXXV.

QUESTIONS OF LAW AND APPEALS.

1. When a Commissioner desires to submit a question of law for the hearing and determination of a Judicial Commissioner, he may by ruling refer the proceedings before him to a Judicial Commissioner for the purpose of having the question determined, or, in a case signed by him, state the question of law he requires to have determined; and he shall give such directions as to the service of notice as he may deem necessary. *Submission of question of law by a Commissioner.*

Appeal on question of law: notice of.

2. An appeal from the decision of a Commissioner acting alone shall, if the appeal be on a question of law, be brought by notice of motion within fourteen days from the date of such decision. The notice shall state the name of the Commissioner whose decision is appealed against, and shall be served upon all parties directly affected by the appeal, and it shall not be necessary to serve parties not so affected.

Judicial Commissioner may direct notices to be served.

3. A Judicial Commissioner may direct notice of appeal, or an application to determine a question of law, to be served on all or any parties to the proceedings, or upon any person not a party, and in the meantime he may postpone or adjourn the hearing upon such terms as may be just; and he may give such judgment and make such order as might have been given or made if the persons served with such notice had been originally parties.

Requisition to have order of a Commissioner and made on question of law reconsidered by three Commissioners.

4. A requisition to have the order of a Commissioner not made upon a question of law reconsidered by a Judicial Commissioner and two other Commissioners shall be in Form 33, and shall be lodged in the Registrar's Office within fourteen days from the date of such order. The requisition shall be laid before a Judicial Commissioner who, if he thinks it desirable that the case should be reheard, shall direct a notice to be served as provided by Rule 2 of this Order.

Amendment of notice of appeal.

5. Any notice of appeal may be amended at any time as a Judicial Commissioner may think fit. Additional evidence may be used on the hearing of the appeal or on the reconsideration of the order of a Commissioner when an order giving liberty to do so has been made on a special application for that purpose to a Judicial Commissioner.

ORDER XXXVI.

SALE BY A LANDLORD TO A TENANT IN CONSIDERATION OF A FINE AND A RENTCHARGE.

Form of agreement.

1. An agreement between landlord and tenant for the sale and purchase of a holding in consideration of the tenant paying a fine, and engaging to pay the vendor a rentcharge, with application for an advance may be in Form 10, with the following addition after "fee-simple" in clause 1 of the agreement, viz.:—" in consideration of a fine of £   , and of a perpetual yearly rentcharge of £   , which the said tenant hereby engages to pay."

Application for further advance for redemption of rentcharge.

2. An application for a further advance for the redemption of the rentcharge shall be by agreement between the owner of the rentcharge and the registered owner of the holding for the sale and purchase of the rentcharge, with application for an advance, and shall be in such form as the Land Commission may from time to time direct.

ORDER XXXVII.

PURCHASE BY A TENANT FROM THE LAND JUDGES.

1. The application by a tenant for an advance to enable him to purchase his holding from the Land Judges shall be in Form 34, or such other form as the Land Commission may from time to time direct. The application shall be on stout writing medium paper, and endorsed with the county, title of the matter, and tenant's name, and shall be signed and verified by the tenant or by some person acting under a power of attorney from him. The application shall be prepared in accordance with the directions in that behalf annexed to the Form.

2. With such application there shall be lodged a copy of the Court rental.

3. If a number of tenants on the same estate are purchasing, the applications should, when practicable, be all lodged together, and may be lodged by the person having carriage of the proceedings before the Land Judges.

ORDER XXXVIII.

PURCHASE OF ESTATES BY THE LAND COMMISSION FOR RE-SALE, AND NEGOTIATIONS OF SALES BY THE LAND COMMISSION.

1. No application to the Land Commission to purchase an estate the subject matter of proceedings before the Land Judges for resale to the tenants shall be entertained unless a Land Judge shall certify that sales to the occupying tenants cannot conveniently be effected unless the Land Commission purchase such estate.

2. The person making the application shall lodge in the Agreements for Purchase Office a copy of the Court rental and undertakings by the several tenants to buy their respective holdings in Form 35, specifying the prices they propose to pay and the amounts of the advances they require.

3. When a landlord desires to sell his estate to the Land Commission for the purpose of re-sale to the tenants, and has lodged an originating statement, he may make application to the Land Commission in Form 30, and he shall satisfy the Commissioner that a competent number of the tenants are able and willing to purchase their holdings, and shall obtain from a competent number of the tenants, undertakings to purchase their holdings, which may be in Form 35, with such variation as may be necessary.

4. When the prescribed number of tenants on any estate desire that the Land Commission shall purchase an estate for re-sale to them, they shall lodge undertakings in Form 35, with such variations as may be necessary, and they shall also lodge such sum as the Commissioner may require, to cover the expenses of negotiation and valuation.

Negotiation of sales by the Land Commission.

5. When either landlord or tenant desires the sale to be negotiated and completed through the medium of the Land Commission, an application for that purpose may be made in the Agreements for Purchase Office, and the Commissioner may entertain the application, provided the party applying undertakes to pay the necessary expenses of such negotiation.

ORDER XXXIX.

SALES UNDER SECTION 40 OF THE LAND LAW (IRELAND) ACT, 1896.

Matter to be referred to Commissioners in rotation.

1. Where a request is issued to the Land Commission by the Land Judge, under the provisions of section 40, sub-section 1, of the Land Law (Ireland) Act, 1896, the matter shall be submitted to two Commissioners (other than the Judicial Commissioner) in such rotation as the Land Commission shall from time to time direct.

Inspection.

2. The subject of such request shall then be referred by such two Commissioners to an Inspector (being the Resident Inspector or one of the Assistant Commissioners) to report in such form and as to such matters as the Land Commission may from time to time direct.

Reference in case of difference.

3. In the event of two Commissioners not agreeing as to the report to be made to the Land Judge in pursuance of such request the submission to them shall stand discharged, and thereupon the matter shall be submitted to two Commissioners (of whom one at least shall not be one of those to whom the matter was originally submitted) in such rotation as the Land Commission may from time to time direct; and such two Commissioners may act on any report of an Inspector in the matter already made, or may require such further inspection or report as to them shall seem fit.

Power to transfer under special circumstances.

4. Where owing to special circumstances it may appear desirable, the Judicial Commissioner may transfer the matter from the Commissioners to whom under Rule 1 hereof it would stand referred to such other two Commissioners as he shall think fit.

ORDER XL.

PRELIMINARY EXPENSES.

If it shall appear to the Commissioner necessary to make a survey or a preliminary inquiry in respect of any application, he may, before entertaining it, require the applicant to lodge such sum as he may consider sufficient to cover the reasonable expenses of such survey or inquiry; and the Commissioner may require such statements, rentals, or other documents to be furnished and verified, as he may think fit.

ORDER XLI.

Proceedings under the Redemption of Rent (Ireland) Act, 1891.

1. An application by a lessee or grantee to redeem his rent pursuant to section 1 of the Redemption of Rent (Ireland) Act, 1891, or, in the alternative, to be deemed a tenant of a present tenancy and to have a fair rent fixed shall be made by originating notice on foolscap paper in Form 37, which shall bear an impressed stamp of the value of one shilling, and shall be served upon the lessor or grantor in the manner provided by the rules in force for the time being in relation to proceedings under the Land Law Acts as regards the service of such notices upon landlords. When such notice shall have been served, the original thereof, with the service or services endorsed thereon, shall be lodged in the Land Commission. *Application to be by originating notice; service of.*

2. The lessor or grantor may within two months from the service on him of the originating notice, lodge in the Land Commission a consent to such redemption, on stout writing medium paper in Form 38; and he shall transmit a notice in Form 80 of the lodgment of such consent, by registered letter, addressed to the lessee or grantee at the postal address stated in the originating notice, or, if the lessee or grantee be represented by a solicitor, to such solicitor at his registered place of business. *Consent to redemption.*

3. The originating notice and consent shall be referred to such Commissioner, and in such rotation as the Land Commission may from time to time direct : provided that all originating notices and consents in which the same lessor or grantor is named shall be referred to the Commissioner to whom the first of such originating notices and consents shall have been referred; and provided that if a vendor has lodged an originating statement, all originating notices and consents in which he shall be named as lessor or grantor shall be referred to the Commissioner to whom such statement stands referred, and all subsequent proceedings shall be had in the matter commenced by the lodgment of such statement. The proceedings under every originating notice and consent shall be subject to transfer from one Commissioner to another on the fiat of the Judicial Commissioner as in the case of proceedings under an originating statement. *Reference to a Commissioner.*

4. When the lessee or grantee receives notice of the lodgment of a consent to the redemption, he shall lodge in the Agreements for Purchase Office a map of the holding and evidence of area in accordance with the Rules as to maps to be lodged with agreements for purchase, in so far as such Rules are applicable, and a certificate of the tenement valuation, unless these shall have been already lodged by the lessor or grantor. The lessee *Proceedings towards obtaining conditional order for redemption.*

or grantee shall then enter the application for hearing before the Commissioner upon notice to the lessor or grantor, stating the affidavits and other documents by which he intends to support his application. If the Commissioner is of opinion that the lessee or grantee is *prima facie* entitled to have his rent redeemed, he may make a conditional order for its redemption subject to the general rules applicable to the case being complied with.

Originating statement and title.

5. Within one month from the date of such order the lessor or grantor shall lodge an originating statement and abstract of title, unless the holding be comprised in an originating statement and abstract of title already lodged; and the lessee or grantee shall furnish the Examiner with such evidence of his title to the holding as may be required, and for that purpose he, or his solicitor, shall attend before the Examiner and take his directions.

Application for an advance.

6. The lessee or grantee may, within fourteen days from the date of the conditional order for redemption, lodge an application for an advance of the whole or any portion of the redemption money, which application shall be on foolscap paper in Form 40; and shall be verified by the affidavit of the lessee or grantee.

Notification to incumbrancers and others interested.

7. If a notice of the filing of the originating statement has been served, the conditional order for redemption shall be notified in the same manner as is prescribed for the notification of the conditional sanction of sales. If the originating statement only comprises the lessee's or grantee's holding a notice in Form 41 shall be substituted for the notice of filing.

Proceedings towards fixing fair rent in event of consent not being lodged or of delay.

8. If the lessor or grantor does not lodge a consent to the redemption within the prescribed time, or if the Commissioner makes an order declaring that the lessor or grantor has caused unreasonable delay in carrying the redemption into effect, the originating notice shall be dealt with as an application by the lessee or grantee to be deemed a tenant of a present tenancy, and have a fair rent fixed; and all subsequent proceedings shall be had thereon as if the originating notice had been served by a lessee under the Land Law Acts; and the lessee or grantee shall, if the Poor Law valuation of the holding is not under £10, within twenty-one days from the expiration of the time within which the consent might have been lodged, or from the making of such order as aforesaid, serve upon the lessor or grantor the particulars of any improvements in respect of which evidence is intended to be produced, or which are intended to be relied on by the lessee or grantee as having been made by him or his predecessors in title, with the dates at which the same were made, according to the best of the lessee's or grantee's knowledge or belief. The Court may, on special grounds, make an order that particulars shall be given when the valuation is under £10.

ORDER XLII.

ENTITLING AND FILING OF DOCUMENTS.

1. All statements, notices, orders, affidavits, consents, under- Entitling. takings, certificates and other documents for the purpose of any motion or proceeding, including proceedings for redemption under the Redemption of Rent (Ireland) Act, 1891, shall, unless otherwise directed by Rule, be headed "Court of the Irish Land Commission—Land Purchase Acts," and be endorsed with the Record Number, and shall be entitled " In the Matter of the Estate of A.B., a Vendor of Land," or, if the Vendor or Vendors be a trustee or trustees for sale or with power of sale, " In the Matter of the Estate of A.B. and C.D., trustees for sale (or, with power of sale) under the Will dated   of E.F. deceased (or, of the Estate of E.F. under Indenture dated   ), Vendors of Land."

2. All affidavits, consents, undertakings, and notices shall be Filing. fairly written or printed on foolscap paper, with sufficient margin, and filed in the Registrar's Office.

ORDER XLIII.

CERTIFIED COPIES AND PRODUCTION OF DOCUMENTS.

1. Copies of affidavits or of statements of facts made by the Certified copies. parties filing the same shall be compared and certified free of charge, if they are lodged along with the originals and are fairly and accurately written. Save as aforesaid, certified copies of affidavits, orders, and other documents filed or lodged in the Land Commission shall be made in the office and certified by an officer of the proper department. Such copies shall (save where otherwise provided) be charged for at the rate of three half-pence per folio of seventy-two words; provided that the minimum charge shall be 3d. Copies of agreements for purchase and of Inspectors' Reports shall be furnished at a uniform charge of 1s. each. All payments for copies shall be denoted by Land Commission stamps.

2. No certified copy shall be issued without the leave of a Copies of certain documents and Commissioner of any abstract of title or document connected to issue without therewith, or of any conveyance to a tenant, or vesting order, leave. nor shall a certified copy of an agreement for purchase between vendor and purchaser be issued without the like leave except to the vendor or purchaser or their respective solicitors.

3. If any person requires the production of any deed or docu- Production of ment in the custody of the Land Commission on the trial of any records in other action, or the hearing of any civil bill, cause, or matter, or in any courts. other legal proceedings, civil or criminal, and it is necessary that an officer of the Land Commission should attend to produce the same, application should be made to a Commissioner. The Secretary, or, in his absence, the Keeper of the Records, shall arrange what officer shall attend.

D

ORDER XLIV.

SOLICITORS.

To attend in person for certain business.

1. Solicitors shall attend in person on the following occasions:—

(a.) On all motions before a Commissioner.

(b.) When discharging requisitions on title before an Examiner.

(c.) On the settlement and vouching of allocation schedules.

(d.) When applying to an Examiner for directions, or for a certificate, or report.

May be represented by Dublin agent or registered clerk.

2. In any of the above cases, however, when a solicitor is unavoidably absent, he may be represented by his Dublin agent, being a registered solicitor, or by his own or his Dublin agent's registered apprentice, or competent registered clerk.

Registered apprentice or clerk.

3. For the purposes aforesaid, any solicitor desirous of employing an apprentice or clerk for transacting business, shall sign a certificate, stating the name of such apprentice or clerk, and that he is a fit and competent person to transact such business, and undertaking to be responsible for the acts of such apprentice or clerk in the ordinary transaction of business. Such certificate shall be in Form 42, and on being produced to the Keeper of Records the same shall be entered in a book to be called "The Clerks' Registry Book," and such apprentice or clerk shall be considered as the representative of the solicitor for the purpose of the proceedings until the same shall be revoked by such solicitor; such revocation shall be entered in "The Clerks' Registry Book."

Every solicitor shall be responsible to the Court for the acts of his registered apprentice or clerk in the ordinary transaction of business.

Every registered apprentice or clerk shall be bound, if called upon so to do by any officer of the Court, to produce a certificate of his registration, signed by the Keeper of Records in Form 43.

Suspension of solicitors.

4. Any solicitor may be suspended or prohibited from practising before the Land Commission by order of a Commissioner.

ORDER XLV.

DELAY IN CONDUCT OF PROCEEDINGS.

Duty of person having carriage of proceedings to prosecute same.

1. No agreement for purchase shall be withdrawn without the leave of the Commissioner; nor shall the several proceedings therein be stayed or delayed beyond the time at which the same respectively might be taken without the sanction of the Commissioner; and it shall be the duty of the person having the carriage of any proceedings or his solicitor to prosecute the same

with due diligence and effect, according to the course of the Court, and to take the Commissioner's directions upon any cause of delay which may arise.

2. The Commissioner shall from time to time investigate the state of each matter and the proceedings therein; and if any case appears not to have been prosecuted with due diligence, the person having the carriage of the proceedings or his solicitor shall be required by notice in writing to attend before the Commissioner to explain the reason of the delay. The Commissioner may, if he think fit, transfer the carriage to some other party interested, or may dismiss the proceedings, and in either case may make such order as may seem right as to costs, and may order the transfer of all papers and documents connected with the case.

May be summoned to explain delay.

ORDER XLVI.

Costs.

1. The Commissioner shall have full power and discretion as to the giving or withholding of costs and expenses, and as to the persons by whom, and the funds out of which the same shall in the first instance, or ultimately be paid, repaid, or borne, and may apportion the same amongst such parties, and in respect of interest, rents, or income, and principal, or corpus, as they shall think fit.

Commissioner have power to give and withhold.

2. When preliminary expenses have been incurred in the negotiation of the terms of sale, the Commissioner may, if he thinks fit, allow as part of the costs in the matter such sum to cover the expenses of such negotiations as he shall consider reasonable.

Expenses of negotiating sales.

3. In all cases in which the Commissioner shall award costs to any party, he may by order direct payment of a sum in gross in lieu of taxed costs, and also direct by and to whom such sum in gross shall be paid.

Commissioner may award gross sum in lieu of taxed costs.

4. In the absence of any agreement to the contrary between a solicitor and his client, the costs incurred in the course of proceedings in the Land Commission under the Land Purchase Acts, shall be taxed according to Part I. of the schedule of fees in the appendix hereto; such costs shall, unless the proceeds of the sales be paid into the High Court, be taxable by the Solicitor to the Land Commission on notice to such persons as the Examiner shall certify. The certificate of such Solicitor shall be final if not varied by the Commissioner.

Costs to be taxed in accordance with Part I. of schedule of fees, and on notice.

5. The costs of any proceeding which is delayed beyond the time limited therefor by any rule or order shall not be allowed on taxation without the direction of the Commissioner.

Costs of delayed proceeding not to be allowed except by order.

6. No costs shall be allowed in respect of the service or publication of any notice, order, or other document, where the copy served or published does not correspond with the original.

If document served be inaccurate no costs to be allowed.

D 2

No costs of supplemental originating statement or of an amendment to be allowed except by order.

7. No costs of a supplemental originating statement, or of the amendment of an originating statement shall be allowed without the direction of the Commissioner.

Costs of abstract of title to be certified for.

8. The Examiner shall certify on the back of the abstract of title whether the whole, or any and what portion of the costs thereof should be allowed; and such allowance shall, (unless otherwise expressed in the certificate,) refer as well to the readings as to the abstract itself. The officer taxing such costs shall have regard to such certificate unless it be varied by the Commissioner. The costs of a supplemental abstract of title shall be taxed as if the additional matter had been embodied in the original abstract, unless the Examiner certifies that separate costs are to be allowed.

Costs of affidavits, &c., used for title or to vouch services, &c.

9. If the costs of any affidavit or other document used for the discharge of requisitions on title, or in proof of services, publications, or postings, are to be allowed on taxation, the Examiner, or other officer whose duty it shall be to read such affidavit or other document shall so certify on the back thereof.

Costs of agreements for purchase may be disallowed.

10. It shall be the duty of the Examiner when settling the draft vesting order, or certifying that the agreement for purchase may be fiated, to disallow the whole or some portion of the costs of any agreement for purchase which he considers has not been prepared with reasonable accuracy, care, and skill; and the taxing officer shall have regard to the Examiner's ruling unless the same be varied by the Commissioner.

Costs of apportionment of quit and crown rent and tithe rent-charge.

11. Except by direction of the Commissioner, no costs shall be allowed of any application for the apportionment of a quit or crown rent or impropriate tithe-rentcharge, unless the Examiner has certified that an apportionment is necessary.

Counsel's fees.

12. Counsel's fees shall not be allowed on the taxation of costs without the direction of the Commissioner.

Costs of owners of superior interests and incumbrancers.

13. Every owner of a superior interest, and every incumbrancer shall have with his demand his costs properly incurred, (including the costs of proving his demand,) unless the Commissioner shall otherwise direct.

Approval of agreement on behalf of tenant.

14. When a purchasing tenant desires that his agreement for purchase shall be approved of by a solicitor on his behalf, such solicitor shall be entitled to charge the tenant for such approval, including all attendances and perusals incident thereto, a fee of 10s. 6d. where the purchase-money shall not exceed £300, and a fee of £1 1s. where the purchase-money exceeds £500.

Costs of vesting orders in cases contracted before 16th August, 1896.

15. The costs of vesting orders in proceedings to which the provisions of Part III. of the Land Law (Ireland) Act, 1896, as to a vesting order do not apply and in which more than one holding shall be vested by a single order shall be taxed in accordance with Part II. of the said schedule of fees, and it shall be the duty of the Examiner to disallow the whole, or some part of the

costs of any vesting order the draft of which shall not have been prepared with reasonable care and skill. The taxing officer shall have regard to any ruling or certificate of an Examiner as to costs endorsed upon a draft vesting order, unless the same shall have been varied by the Commissioner.

If in any matter, by reason of the vendor or his solicitor not having exercised due diligence in the collection of interest on purchase money, or conduct of the proceedings, more vesting orders are lodged than would otherwise have been necessary, the costs of such additional vesting orders shall be taxed as if the holdings had been included in the first vesting order made in the matter; provided that if the delay shall have been caused by the default of the vendor, the solicitor shall be entitled to be paid the difference between the reduced costs and the full costs by the vendor, or out of any portion of the proceeds of the sales payable to him. It shall be the duty of the Examiner to certify on the drafts of such additional vesting orders whether the full costs are to be allowed or not, and whether any costs are to be chargeable against the vendor personally.

ORDER XLVII.

Proceedings for Recovery of Costs.

1. In every case in which the Court shall award costs to be paid by any person, the person to whom such costs shall have been awarded or his solicitor may, on application to the Registrar, obtain a writ of *fieri facias* to enforce payment of such costs in Form 44.

2. The person so applying must produce to the Registrar the order awarding the costs, the certificate of their taxation unless they shall have been measured by the Court, and a certificate by the solicitor for the applicant or by the applicant that the costs have been demanded and have not been paid.

3. A sum of ten shillings and sixpence may be added to such costs for the costs of and incident to the issue of the writ.

ORDER XLVIII.

Order to Sheriff to put Purchaser into Possession.

1. When a holding is sold by or at the suit of the Land Commission, the purchaser may at any time within one month after the execution of his conveyance or vesting order obtain by side-bar motion an order for the sheriff to put him in possession of such lands or any part thereof upon production to the Registrar of an affidavit in Form 45. A purchaser requiring an order for possession after the expiration of the said period must apply to the Commissioner for such order. The order may be in Form 46.

Order for possession may be made before conveyance or vesting order.

2. The Commissioner may, if he think fit, make an order for possession before the execution of the conveyance or vesting order to the purchaser, or notwithstanding that the purchaser shall not have made any demand of possession.

ORDER XLIX.

APPLICATION THAT ANNUITY BE NOT REDUCED AT END OF DECADE.

Application that annuity be not reduced.

The application by the proprietor of a holding charged with an annuity that the annuity payable during the ensuing decade shall not be reduced, shall be in writing addressed to the Secretary of the Land Commission, and shall be accompanied by the receipt for the last payment of the annuity. Such application shall be made not less than one month prior to the end of the current decade.

ORDER L.

RETENTION OF LAND CERTIFICATE BY LAND COMMISSION.

Lodgment of application for advance to imply consent to retention of land certificate.

1. The lodgment with the Land Commission of an application for an advance shall imply a consent by the applicant that the land certificate issued on the first registration of the purchaser's ownership of the holding, and any further or other land certificate issued in substitution therefor on transfer or transmission of the interest in the holding, shall be delivered by the Registering Authority to the Land Commission and retained by them so long as any money remains due in respect of the purchase annuity.

Copy to be issued to owner.

2. A copy of any land certificate so retained shall be issued by the Land Commission free of charge to the registered owner of the holding.

ORDER LI.

LETTERS ON OFFICIAL BUSINESS.

Letters on official business.

All letters on official business other than letters to the Solicitor of the Commission, shall be addressed to the Secretary, Irish Land Commission, Dublin, and not to a Commissioner or other officer of the Land Commission.

Seal of the Irish Land Commission.

Signed,

E. T. BEWLEY.
S. J. LYNCH.
FRED. WRENCH.
GERALD FITZGERALD.

APPENDIX.

FORM 1.

ORIGINATING STATEMENT.

COURT OF THE IRISH LAND COMMISSION.

LAND PURCHASE ACTS.

RECORD No. ,

In the matter of the Estate of *A.B.* a Vendor of Land.

The statement of the said *A.B.* of   in the County of

SHOWETH :

1. That the said *A.B.* is owner of the lands described in the First   *If there are*
Schedule hereto, which lands are held by the tenure therein stated, and   *more vendors*
that he is now and has been in possession of and in receipt of the rents   *than one their*
and profits of the said lands since the year 18   .   *estate and interests must be specified.*

Variation where the Vendor is Tenant for Life.

[1. That the said *A.B.* is owner as tenant for life of the lands described
in the First Schedule hereto, which lands are held by the tenure therein
stated, and that he is now and has been in possession of and in receipt of
the rents and profits of the said lands since the year 18   .

That   of   is entitled to the next estate in the said lands in
remainder expectant upon the determination of the said life estate.

That   of   and   of   are Trustees *with power of*   (a) Settlement
sale of the said lands under the (a)   dated the   day of   *or Will.*
18   b).   (b) Here describe instrument.

(*If there is no power of sale, and the Trustees were appointed for the*
purposes of the Settled Land Acts, 1882 to 1890, state so.)]

Variation where the Vendors are Trustees for Sale.

[1. That the said *A.B.* and *C.D.* are owners as trustees for sale of the   (c) Here state
lands described in the First Schedule hereto, which lands are held by the   *names and*
tenure therein stated, and that   of   is now and has been   *addresses, and*
as far as
in possession of and in receipt of the rents and profits of the said lands   *possible the*
since the year 18   , and that the persons beneficially entitled to the   *respective*
shares of the
proceeds of the sale thereof are (c).]   *parties.*

56

Variation where the Vendors are Trustees with power of Sale.

[1. That the said *A. B.* and *C.D.* are trustees with a power of sale of the lands described in the First Schedule hereto with the consent in writing of *E.F.* of   in the County of   , which lands are held by the tenure therein stated. That the said *E.F.* is owner as tenant for life (or *otherwise*) of the said lands, and has been in possession of and in receipt of the rents and profits of the said lands since the year 18   . That   of   is entitled to the next estate in the said lands in remainder expectant upon the determination of the said life estate.]

Variation where the Vendor is a Mortgagee in possession with power of Sale.

[1. That the said *A.B.* is mortgagee in possession with power of sale of the lands described in the First Schedule hereto under an Indenture of Mortgage dated the   day of   18   , from *C.D.* to the said *A.B.*, which lands are held by the tenure in the said Schedule stated. That the said *A.B.* entered into possession of the said lands as mortgagee on the   day of   18   , and has so continued to the present time. That *E.F.*, of   in the County of   , is entitled to the equity of redemption in the said lands under the said Indenture of mortgage.]

(d) Here state when and under what instrument or how he became entitled; a copy of the instrument must be lodged if required.

2. That the said *A.B.* became entitled as such owner as aforesaid under the   dated the   day of   18   . (d)

3. That the said *A.B.* has set forth in the said First Schedule the particulars of all superior interests as defined by Section 31 of the Land Law (Ireland) Act, 1896, [save such rentcharges and annuities as are incumbrances on the lands and are set forth in the Second Schedule hereto] which he knows, or believes, to affect the said lands, and, so far as the same are known to him, the dates of, and parties to the instruments (if any) creating such superior interests, and the names and addresses of the persons entitled thereto.

Variation if there are no Superior Interests.

[3. That there are no superior interests as defined by Section 31 of the Land Law ([Ireland) Act, 1896, affecting the said lands.]

4. That all the charges and incumbrances [other than the charges hereinbefore referred to] affecting the said lands are fully set forth in the Second Schedule hereto.

Variation if the Lands be Unincumbered.

[4. That there are no charges or incumbrances [other than the charges hereinbefore referred to] affecting the said lands.]

5. That there are not any proceedings pending in any Court of
Justice in relation to the said lands or any part thereof or to the
receipt of the rents and profits thereof and that no person interested
therein is an infant, idiot, lunatic, or married woman save (e).

6. That the said A. B. contemplates selling the said lands or some
parts thereof under the Land Purchase Acts, in fee-simple, freed and
discharged from all superior interests and incumbrances save (f) (and
requires the title to the residue of the said lands to be investigated for
purposes of registration under the "Local Registration of Title (Ireland)
Act, 1891.")

[7. That C. D. of   is the land agent of A. B. and in receipt
of the rents and profits of the said lands on his behalf, and the said A. B.
is desirous that any interest payable under section 3b sub-section (2) of
the Land Law (Ireland) Act, 1896, shall be paid to the said C. D. (g).]

8. And the said A. B. desires that this statement shall be received
by the Irish Land Commission as the basis for carrying out the said
intended sales, and that he may have such further aid and relief incidental to such sales as the nature of the case may require, according to
the judgment of the Court.

Signature of Vendor, ———

(e) Here state
the names of
persons (if any)
exempted, and
the names and
addresses of, as
the case may be,
the Guardian of
the Infant, Com-
mittee of Luna-
tic, or Husband
of Married
Woman.
(f) Have inserct
the particulars
of any superior
interests which
it is intended
the sale shall be
made subject to.
(g) To be in-
serted when
vendor desires
interest under
agreements to
be paid to agent.

First Schedule referred to in the foregoing Statement.

Barony and Townland (Ordnance Survey Names), Parish, Barony and County.	Quantity of Lands, Statute Measure, of each denomination.	Total number of Tenants on each denomination.	Total of Rents payable by Tenants on each denomination.	Tenement Valuation of each denomination.	Tenure by which the lands are held and particulars of Superior Interests (viz. any rent, fees, duties, or services, payable or to be rendered in respect of the lands, and any customs, exceptions, reservations, covenants, conditions, or agreements contained in any Fee-farm Grant, or other Conveyance in Fee, or Lease under which the lands are held, and any reversion or estate expectant on the determination of such lease, or of any term of years for which the lands are held), and dates of said parties to the instruments creating such Superior Interests, and names and addresses of the persons entitled thereto.	Observations.
	A. R. P.		£ s. d.	£ s. d.		

Note.—The 2nd, 3rd, 4th, and 5th columns must be accurately totted.

Signature of Vendor, ———

*If the root of title to any denomination is a Conveyance or Declaration
of Title by the Incumbered Estates Court, Landed Estates Court, or Land
Judges' Court, the date of such Conveyance or Declaration of Title should
be given in the observation column. If the Lands are not held in Fee
Simple, the date and particulars of the Grant or Lease under which they
are held should be given. If any denomination cannot be sold under the
Land Purchase Acts by reason of the vendor not being the immediate
landlord of the occupying tenants, it is desirable that there should be a
statement in the observation column to that effect, and to the effect that
the lands in question are excluded from the proceedings: otherwise they
will be included in the public notices.*

58

Second Schedule referred to in the foregoing Statement.

Date of Incumbrance.	Name and Address of Incumbrancer.	Particulars of Incumbrance.	Sum due for Principal.	Arrears of Interest or Annuity to last gale day.	Special circumstances (if any) relating to each Incumbrance.
			£ s. d.	£ s. d.	

Note.—The 4th and 5th columns must be separately totted.

Signature of Vendor, ———

This Schedule should state concisely the manner in which the charge was created, whether by will, settlement, mortgage, judgment, or otherwise, and by whom. If the Incumbrances have been consolidated this should be stated, and any special circumstances, such, for example, as the terms on which an Incumbrance may be paid off or an annuity redeemed, or any exemption of a portion of the lands from the whole or any portion of the Incumbrance, or the liability of any other property or of any person to pay any Incumbrance, whether in exoneration of the lands or otherwise. If there are Incumbrances on the life estate they should be stated separately, thus:—1st part, Incumbrances on the Fee; 2nd part, Incumbrances on the Life Estate.

Affidavit.

I, *A.B.*, the Vendor make Oath and say:

That I have read the foregoing Statement and the Schedules annexed thereto, and I say that the said Statement and Schedules are true and correct in every particular to the best of my knowledge, information, and belief; and I further say that there is not any person to my knowledge or belief who has or claims any estate, right, title, or interest in the said lands or any part thereof save as in the said statement is set forth.

Sworn, &c.

FORM 2.

NOTICE of the FILING of an ORIGINATING STATEMENT.

Heading and Title as before.

Sir,—Take notice that on the   day of   189 , an Originating Statement was filed on behalf of the said vendor affecting lands in the Barony of   and County of   , which it is contemplated selling under the Land Purchase Acts in fee-simple, freed and discharged from all superior interests as defined by section 31 of the Land Law (Ireland) Act, 1896, save (a)   and from all other charges and incumbrances, and that your name appears in such statement as entitled to [*here state the nature of the superior interest, charge, incumbrance, or other estate or interest in which the person is entitled*], and that your postal address is stated to be

(a) Here insert the particulars of any superior interests which is to intended the sale shall be made subject to.

to which address will be sent, as long as the Commissioner shall consider it necessary for the due protection of your rights, a notification of the conditional sanction of all sales of the said lands to the tenants, and such other notices in reference thereto as the Commissioner may direct. And further take notice that if no application to the contrary be made by you, by motion to the Commissioner upon notice to me, within fourteen days from the date of such notification, the sales will be completed in due course without further notice to you.

Dated this   day of   189 .

Solicitor for the Vendor.

[Registered address.]

To

N.B.—Should your name or address be incorrectly stated above, you should fill up the annexed form and transmit it at once to the Land Commission. Should you desire the notification to be sent to a solicitor on your behalf, or that you should have notice of all further proceedings, you should instruct your solicitor to enter an appearance for you, and have the notifications sent to him.

Heading and Title as before.

I request that you will have the Register amended as follows, in respect of the matters referred to in the Notice of Filing of Originating Statement served on me.

Name at present registered.	Name of person to whom notifications are to be sent
Postal address at present registered.	Postal address within the United Kingdom.
	If above person be an agent, state name of principal.

Dated this   day of   189

(Signature.)

To the Secretary,
    Irish Land Commission,
        24, Upper Merrion-street, Dublin.

Form 3.

General Notice to Claimants.

Heading and Title as before.

Whereas an Originating Statement has, on the   day of 189 , been filed affecting the lands of   containing statute measure or thereabouts, situate in the Barony of and County of   , Let All Persons Take Notice that the said Vendor contemplates selling the said lands or some part thereof under the Land Purchase Acts, and that such sale will be made in fee-simple freed from and discharged from all superior interests, as defined by section 31 of the Land Law (Ireland) Act, 1896, save (a).   and from all other charges and incumbrances. And Let all Persons having claims on the said lands Take Notice that they may enter appearances in the said matter for the purpose of being served with notice of the proceedings.

(a) Here insert the particulars of any superior interests which it is intended the sale shall be made subject to.

Dated this   day of   189 .

Examiner

Solicitor for the Vendor,

Dublin.

Form 4.

Notice and Requisition to Quit Rent Office.

Heading and Title as before.

Take notice, that an Originating Statement has been this day filed affecting the lands specified in the Schedule herein, and that sales of such lands may be carried into effect by vesting order and made discharged from all superior interests as defined by sect. 31 of the Land Law (Ireland) Act, 1896. I have to request that you will be good enough to state, for the information of the Court, on the duplicate sent herewith, whether the particulars of the rents payable to Her Majesty in respect of such lands are correctly specified in the said Schedule, and return the same to the Registrar at your earliest convenience.

Dated this   day of   189 .

Solicitor for the Vendor.

To the Superintendent of the Quit Rent Office,

—— Dublin,

on behalf of the Commissioners of Her
Majesty's Woods Forests and Land
Revenues.

Schedule referred to in the foregoing Notice.

Barony, Townland, Ordnance Survey Sheet, Number, and County.	Area. Statute Measure.	No. of Ordnance Sheet on which shown.	Quit or Crown Rent paid.	Name of Original Crown Patentee, and date of Patent.	Tenure by which Lands are held by Vendor.	Name of person in receipt of Head Rent, if any be payable.	Date of Conveyance or Declaration of Title (if any) by Incumbered Estates, Landed Estates, or Land Judges' Courts, name of Grantee, and title of matter in which such Conveyance or Declaration was made.
	A. R. P.		£				

Note.—All the columns of the Schedule must be filled in, and should correspond with the Originating Statement in so far as the particulars required are therein stated. If the particulars to be specified in the 4th column are not known the words " not known " should be inserted therein. If there be no head rent payable, or if the lands have not been the subject of a conveyance or declaration of title by the Incumbered Estates, Landed Estates, or Land Judges Court, the word " none " should be inserted in the 7th and 8th columns respectively.

62

FORM 5.

NOTICE AND REQUISITION TO BOARD OF PUBLIC WORKS.

Heading and Title as before.

Take notice, that an originating statement has been this day filed affecting the lands specified in the schedule hereto, and that sales of such lands may be made discharged from all superior interests, as defined by section 31 of the Land Law (Ireland) Act, 1896.

I have to request that you will be good enough to state, for the information of the Court, whether the lands are situate within a drainage district, and also the particulars of such charges (if any) as affect the said lands under any of the following Acts, viz.:—

Land Improvement,	. .	10 Victoria, c. 32, and Acts amending the same.
Arterial Drainage,	. .	5 and 6 Victoria, c. 89, and Acts amending the same.
Piers and Harbours,	. .	9 and 10 Victoria, c. 3, and Act amending the same.
Relief of Distress,	. .	43 Victoria, c. 4.
Land Law (Ireland) Act), 1881, 44 and 45 Victoria, c. 49, sections 19 and 31.		

In the event of any portion of the lands being subject to a charge under any of the said Acts, you are requested to state in the observation column of the said schedule if your Board requires notice of the conditional sanction of the advances or agreements for purchase in respect of the lands so charged.

Dated this   day of   189 .

Solicitor for the Vendor.

To

The Accountants of the Board of Public Works.

Schedule referred to in the foregoing requisition.

Townlands, Barony and County (Ordnance Survey Names).	Area Statute Measure.	Tenure by which the lands are held by the Vendor.	Date of Instrument creating charge.	Nature of Instrument.	Act under which charge was made.	Amount of Loan.	Half-yearly Instalment.	Term of Expiry.	Name of person to whom Instalment was made, and observations.
A. R. P.						£ s. d.	£ s. d.		

N.B.—The vendor or his solicitor must fill up the first three columns, and be responsible for their accuracy. If part only of any townland be included in the originating statement, the words "part of" must be inserted before the name of such townland in the above schedule.

Form 7.

Certificate for Registering a Lis Pendens.

To the Registrar of Judgments. (Under 7 & 8 Vic., c. 90.)

Sir,—The following Memorandum or Minute contains the particulars of a Lis Pendens in the Court of the Irish Land Commission, which I require to be registered pursuant to the Statute.

Form of Habitum with the name of the person for whom he is concerned.

Name of the person whose estate is intended to be affected thereby.	Usual or last known place of abode of such person.	Title, trade, or profession of such person.

In the Court of the Irish Land Commission.

Land Purchase Acts.

Title of the Matter,

Record No.

In the Matter of the Estate of

Vendor of Land.

Date of filing Originating Statement, the   day of   189 .

I certify that the Lis Pendens described in the above memorandum or minute is now in existence.

Dated this   day of   189 .

To the Registrar of Judgments

Form 8.

GENERAL CERTIFICATE OF APPEARANCES.

Heading and Title of Matter.

Originating Statement filed   day of   189 .

Name of person appearing.	Address for service, or name of Solicitor and registered place of business.	Nature of Appearance; i.e. "General with notice of motion of Sales," "General without notice of motion of Sales," or "Special for the purpose of, &c."

I certify that the above is a correct abstract of all the Appearances which have been entered in this Matter, being*   appearances in all.   *State the number.

Dated this   day of   , 189 .

Signature, _____

Note.—The above form must be accurately and legibly filled up by the solicitor before lodging it in the Registrar's office.

Form 9.

CERTIFICATE OF THE ENTRY OF AN APPEARANCE.

Heading and Title of Matter.

Name of Person appearing.	Address for service, or name of Solicitor and registered place of business.	Nature of Appearance; i.e. "General with notice of motion of Sales," "General without notice of motion of Sales," or "Special for the purpose of, &c."

I certify that the above is a correct abstract of an Appearance which has been entered in this Matter.

Dated this   day of   , 189 .

Signature, _____

Note.—The above form must be accurately and legibly filled up by the solicitor before lodging it in the Registrar's office.

E

FORM 10.

AGREEMENT FOR SALE BETWEEN VENDOR AND TENANT.

COURT OF THE IRISH LAND COMMISSION.

An Agreement made the ____ day of _____ 189__
between _____ of _____
the Vendor of the holding described in the first part of
the Schedule hereto, and _____ of
_____, the Tenant in occupation of the
said holding.

1. In case the Irish Land Commission shall advance the sum of
£ _____ guaranteed land stock to the said Tenant for the purchase of the said holding, the said Vendor will sell and the said
Tenant will purchase the same in fee-simple, _____

---

at the price of £ _____ *which sum is to include all expenses
incidental to the purchase.*

2. *The balance of the purchase money is to be paid as follows :—
By a Cash Payment by the Tenant of £ _____
By a Mortgage bearing £ ____ per cent. Interest, for £ _____*

3. The Interest on the purchase money payable to the Land
Commission pursuant to Sect. 35, Sub-Sect. 2 of the Land Law (Ireland)
Act, 1896, shall be at the rate of £ (?) ____ per cent. per annum up to
the date of the advance, and at the rate of £3 per cent. per annum from
the date of the advance until the day from which the purchase annuity
begins.

4. The Sale shall be carried out by means of a Vesting Order.

5. The Lodgment of this agreement with the Irish Land Commission
is to be deemed an application by the said Tenant for an advance pursuant
to the Land Purchase Acts, to be repaid as is by the said Acts
provided.

SCHEDULE

County_____ County_____ Electoral Division_____

Item on Map	Admeasurement whereof immediately to commence from	Area Statute Measure of the profit of each Townland to herein	Tenure	Rent paid to Landlord	Terms of Townland profess to bring a note the Landlord to at the...
		First Part—Description of Entry			
		Second Part—admeasurement land and upon the "Purchased Instalment" premises on that entry."		
					If in effect been dealt and ceased to allow estate owners in every cases the instance thereafter to out the houses all the houses on any necessary require the... herein estate to grant	

Signed by the Vendor in presence of

Name_____   Signature of Vendor_____

Address_____   Postal Address_____

Occupation_____

I,_____ the before named Tenant, make oath and say, as follows:—

1. That the particulars stated in the foregoing Schedule are true, to the best of my knowledge and belief.

If a free-term Grant, Lease, or Agreement or the case may be.

"or if not, state to whom possession.

2. I reside on and have been in the occupation of the said holding, and paying the rent therefor since the Year 18___, and I hold the same as Tenant, as in the said Schedule is stated *and the said (*)_____ is in my* possession.

3. There is not any person in occupation of the said holding as Tenant or otherwise save as mentioned in the following Schedule:—

I there are no under-tenants fill in the word "none" where marked * * *

Names of the Persons in occupation as under-tenants or otherwise.	Area in Statute Measure.			Rent (if any) payable by each occupier.			When payable.	Terms or tenure of occupying.
	A.	R.	P.	£	s.	d.		
*	*		*					

4. There is not any charge or incumbrance affecting my interest in the said holding save those specified in the following Schedule:—

If there are no incumbrances, fill in the word "none" where marked thus * * *

Schedule containing particulars of Mortgages, Charges created by deposit of Lease or otherwise, or Charges in favour of the Commissioners of Public Works in Ireland affecting the Tenant's interest in the Holding.			
Date.	Name and Address of Incumbrancer.	Particulars of Incumbrance, Mortgage, or otherwise.	Principal Sum due.
			£ s. d.
	*	*	*

* If the Tenant has previously applied for any advance over "save an advance of £ ... &c.," giving the particulars.

5. I have not obtained from or (except by this Agreement) applied to the Irish Land Commission for an advance of any sum for the purchase of any land,*_____

_____

† If the deponent be illiterate here insert "See 1c."

The words in italics may be struck out unless the deponent be a marksman.

Sworn before me this_____ day of_____ 18__ at_____

in the County of_____ and I know the Deponent. the whole of the foregoing agreement and affidavit having been first read over by† ——— the Deponent who appeared perfectly to understand the same, and made ⟨A⟩——— ⟨mark⟩ *thereto in my presence.*

If the Tenant wishes to be represented in the proceedings by a Solicitor, here insert the name and registered place of business of such Solicitor :—

Name,——   *Address,*——

NOTE.—Section 35 (1) of the Land Law (Ireland) Act, 1896, provides: "Where an agreement for the purchase of a holding is made after the commencement of this Act and is lodged with the Land Commission the purchaser shall, in the event of the sale being carried out, be discharged from all liability to the vendor in respect of any liabilities affecting the holding at the date of the agreement, including all rent and arrears existing at such date ; but if the advance is refused the agreement shall be void, and the tenant shall be liable to pay rent and arrears as if the agreement had not been made. Provided that no proceeding in respect of the said rent and arrears existing at the date of the agreement shall be brought pending the carrying out of the sale."

DIRECTIONS AS TO THE PREPARATION OF THE AGREEMENT AND AFFIDAVIT.

The Agreement and Affidavit must be neatly and accurately prepared, without any blanks, and all clauses not applicable to the case must be struck out, otherwise the Agreement cannot be received.

When females are parties to the Agreement they must be described either as "spinster," "widow," or "wife of A.B."

The price and the advance must be in pounds only.

When it is intended that the Tenant shall pay the stamp duty on his Vesting Order the words "*which sum is to include all expenses incidental to the purchase*" should be struck out.

Clause 1. When additional land is being sold under the "Purchase of Land (Ireland) Amendment Act, 1889," insert after "in fee simple," "together with the additional land specified in the second part of the said schedule." Here also insert any rights of grazing, or turbary, or other rights which are appurtenant to the holding, and which are exercised over lands not included therein, e.g., "together with such right of grazing and cutting turf as has heretofore been exercised by the said Tenant upon the bog on the lands of *Blackacre*, in the possession of the said Vendor [*or if the bog be tenanted* in the occupation of A.B.,] and containing   statute measure or thereabouts." Here also insert any exceptions or reservations coming within sec. 31, sub-sec. 2, of the Land Law (Ireland) Act, 1896, or any superior interests which the vendor and purchaser propose that the sale shall be subject to.

If the advance is of the whole purchase-money strike out clause 2.

In filling up the column headed "Tenure of Tenant," state whether the Tenant holds under Fee-farm Grant (giving date and parties), under Lease or agreement in writing (giving date, parties, and term), under a tenancy from year to year, or how otherwise. If the rent be a Judicial one, state on what date and how it was fixed.

The Agreement must be signed by both Vendor and Tenant, or by some person acting under power of Attorney. An Attorney should sign thus "A.B. by C.D. acting under power of Attorney," *Trustees, or limited owners selling under the provisions of the Settled Land Acts, 1882 to 1890, must themselves sign the agreement.*

The person taking the affidavit should not be the Vendor, his agent, or solicitor, or the Tenant's solicitor.

FORM 11.

NOTICE TO LODGE DEEDS, &c.

Heading and Title of Matter.

You are hereby required, within ten days from the service of this notice upon you, to inform me in writing, whether there are any, and if so, what deeds, leases, counterparts of leases, maps, surveys, rentals, statements of title, or other documents in your custody or power, relating to the estate the subject of the originating statement filed in this matter, or to the charges thereon, namely—

(*Insert particulars.*)

And you are further required, within the same period, to lodge all such documents in this Court.

And you are hereby apprized, that if, having in your custody or power any such documents, you refuse or neglect to comply with this notice, and in consequence thereof an application to the Commissioner may become necessary, this notice will be used to charge you with the costs of such application.

Dated this day of 189 .

To

Solicitor for the Vendor.

FORM 12.

AFFIDAVIT VERIFYING ABSTRACT OF TITLE.

I, of , solicitor for the said vendor, make oath and say :—

1. I have read the foregoing abstract of title previous to swearing this affidavit, and compared the same with the several deeds and documents therein abstracted, so far as they are in the said abstract stated to be forthcoming.

2. The said abstract is a true and correct abstract of title to the lands described at the head thereof, and in the originating statement filed in this matter, and the several documents therein purporting to be abstracted are fairly and correctly abstracted to the best of my knowledge, information, and belief. I have in the schedule of documents intended to be lodged herewith, and indorsed by me, previously to swearing this affidavit, set forth all deeds and muniments of title relating to the said lands which are in my power, possession, or procurement.*

Sworn, &c.

* Here may be added when necessary :—"Except muniments of title having date prior to the root of title, and none of which relate to existing charges or affect the title as abstracted," or, "except documents which have already been lodged in Court in the course of the proceedings herein."

FORM 13.

DRAFT REQUISITION FOR SEARCHES IN THE REGISTRY OF DEEDS.

To the Registrar appointed by Act of Parliament for registering deeds, wills, and so forth in Ireland.

I require (by the direction of the Irish Land Commission) to have an abstract of every memorial registered in the Office for Registering Deeds, and so forth in Ireland, of all acts appearing on a search on the Index of names only, by A.B., from the   day of   18 , to the   day of   18 , by C.D., from the   day of   18 , to the date of making the certificate upon this requisition, &c., to affect the lands of *(follow the rulings on title)*, excepting therefrom the memorials of the following deeds, viz. :—*(Here set out the exceptions consecutively numbered, stating the date and description of each instrument, the parties' names, the date of registration, the book, and the number).*

Dated this   day of   189 ..

G. H., Solicitor for the Vendor.

FORM 14.

DIRECTION FOR SURVEY BY ORDNANCE SURVEY DEPARTMENT.

Heading and Title as before.

Upon application of Mr.   , Solicitor for the said vendor, let it be referred to the Director of the Ordnance Survey Department to survey the lands specified in the schedule hereto, and to furnish a map or maps on a suitable scale, and a report setting forth the names of the several occupying tenants, and the areas of their respective holdings, and also the particulars of the holdings of any sub-tenant of the said occupying tenants, and the names of such sub-tenants.

Dated this   day of   189 ..

Clerk in charge of Agreements
for Purchase Office.

SCHEDULE.

NOTE.—Where whole townlands are to be surveyed the area need not be here stated, but if part only of a townland is to be surveyed the area of such part should be given. The barony and county should always be stated. The description in the schedule should correspond with that in the first schedule to the originating statement.

FORM 15.

AFFIDAVIT VERIFYING OCCUPANCY.

Heading and Title of Matter.

I, of in the county of aged 21 years and upwards, make oath and say :—

1. That the several persons named in the schedule to this affidavit have agreed to purchase their respective holdings in the townlands therein named for the respective sums therein stated.

2. I know the said lands and the occupying tenants thereof, and I say that the said several persons in the said schedule named are still in the occupation of their respective holdings so as aforesaid purchased by them.

3. My means of knowledge of the facts above deposed to are*

Sworn, &c.

SCHEDULE referred to in the foregoing Affidavit.

Townlands (Ordnance Survey Names only to be given).	Name of Tenant Purchaser.	Postal Address of Tenant Purchaser.	Purchase Money.
			£

FORM 16.

THE IRISH LAND COMMISSION—CHURCH PROPERTY DEPARTMENT.

APPLICATION for the APPORTIONMENT of TITHE RENT-CHARGE PAYABLE TO THE IRISH LAND COMMISSION.

Number of the Reemivable Order issued for the rent-charge* } No. (———————)

*Please quote this number correctly.

Diocese ————————

Benefice ————————

Record No. ————————

In the Matter of the Estate of

_____ a Vendor of Land.

WHEREAS the lands mentioned in the first schedule herein are liable to the annual Tithe Rent-charge therein particularly mentioned, payable to the Irish Land Commission. And WHEREAS that part of the said lands mentioned in the first part of the second schedule hereto has been sold pursuant to the provisions of the Land Purchase Acts. Now, I as vendor in this matter apply to the Irish Land Commission that the annual Tithe Rent-charge so chargeable on said lands may be divided and apportioned between the respective parts of said lands so sold and unsold in manner set forth in the second schedule herein.

Dated this ——— day of ——————— 189—.

Signature, ————————

Address, ————————

FIRST SCHEDULE.

Annual Tithe Rent-charge, £ s. d.
Ordnance Survey Names of Townlands, upon which above Rent-charge is charged, Parish and County.

SECOND SCHEDULE.

Townlands included in each Lot.	Contents of each Lot, Statute Measure.	Tenement Valuation of each Lot, exclusive of Buildings.	Amount of Tithe Rent-charge proposed to be charged on each Lot.
	A. R. P.	£ s. d.	£ s. d.
First part—Land sold under Land Purchase Acts.			
Second part—Lands not sold.			
Annual Tithe Rent-charge, as per First Schedule, £			

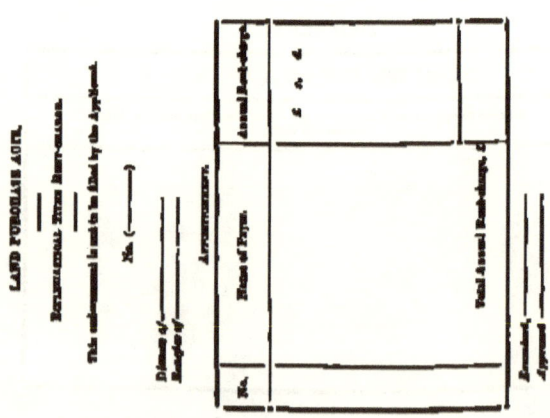

FORM 17.

THE IRISH LAND COMMISSION.—CHURCH PROPERTY DEPARTMENT.

APPLICATION for the APPORTIONMENT of FIXED ANNUAL INSTALMENTS
in lieu of TITHE RENT-CHARGE.

Number of the Receivable
Orders issued for the } No. (——————)
Instalments.*

                                                         * Please quote
this number
correctly.

Diocese ————————

Benefice ————————

Record No. ————

In the Matter of the Estate of   } WHEREAS the lands mentioned
the first schedule hereto are liable
to the annual rent-charge therein
         a Vendor of Land.   particularly mentioned, payable to
The Irish Land Commission for the period of ——————— years
from the First day of ——————— 18—, and charged thereon by
† Merging Order, numbered ——————— bearing date the ——————— day † A certified
of ———————, 188 —. AND WHEREAS that part of said lands copy of the
mentioned in the first part of the second schedule hereto has been sold Merging Order
pursuant to the provisions of the Land Purchase Acts. Now I, as at the office of
vendor in this matter, apply to the Irish Land Commission that the the Irish Land
annual rent-charge so chargeable on said lands may be divided and appor- Commission.
tioned between the respective parts of said lands so sold and unsold in
manner set forth in the second schedule hereto.

Dated this ——— day of ——————— 189 —.

         Signature, ———————————————

         Address, ———————————————

FIRST SCHEDULE.

Fixed Annual Rent-charge, £ : s
Ordnance Survey Names of Townlands, upon which above Rent-charge is charged. Parish and County.

Land Premium Acts,

Third Annual Instalment.

————

(To commence,&c. and to be signed by the Auditor.)

No. (———)

Diocese of ———————————————

Benefice of ———————————————

FORM 18.

STATEMENT OF FACTS FOR THE APPORTIONMENT OF AN IMPROPRIATE
TITHE-RENTCHARGE.

Heading and Title of Matter.

The Statement of Facts of

SHOWETH—

1. That the lands described in the schedule hereto are subject to an annual impropriate tithe-rentcharge of £   s.   d. payable to
of

2. That the said   has been in receipt of the said rentcharge for [six years and upwards] as (*here state whether as owner in fee simple, as tenant for life, as trustee, as lessee under a lease of the rentcharge, or how otherwise. If the person entitled has not been in receipt of the rentcharge for six years, state for what period it has been paid to him*).

3. That [parts of] the lands described in the first part of the said schedule have been sold under the Land Purchase Acts [and it is contemplated selling under the said Acts the residue of such lands, and the same are the property of the said vendor.]

4. That the lands described in the second part of the said schedule are the property of the said vendor, but it is not intended to sell them under the said Acts.

Variation when all the lands are not the property of the vendor.

[4. That the lands described in the second part of the said schedule are not the property of the said vendor, and the name and address of the reputed owner thereof is stated therein.]

5. That save the proceedings herein there is not any suit or matter pending in any Court in relation to the said rentcharge or lands, and that no person hereinbefore referred to is an infant, idiot, lunatic, or married woman [save—*here state the particulars of any suit or matter, and the names of any persons under disability, giving the names and addresses as the case may be of the guardian of infant, committee of lunatic, or husband of married woman.*]

6. That it is expedient that the said rentcharge be apportioned, and the proposed apportionment set forth in the said schedule would be just and fair having regard to the quantities and value of the lands and the rights of the persons interested.

73

SCHEDULE referred to in the foregoing STATEMENT.

Townlands, Parish, Barony and County (Ordnance Survey Names only)	Reference to Map.	Area in Statute Measure of each Townland or part of a Townland.	Tenement Valuation, exclusive of buildings.	Proposed Apportionment.	Observations.
		A. R. P.	£ s. d.	£ s. d.	
		FIRST PART.			
A.—Lands which have been sold.					
B.—Lands which it is contemplated selling.					
		SECOND PART.			
A.—Lands the property of the vendor not intended to be sold.					
B.—Lands the property of	of	in the County of			

I, the above named   , make oath and say that I have read the foregoing statement and the schedule thereto, and the same are true and accurate to the best of my knowledge, information, and belief.

Sworn, etc.

FORM 19.

STATEMENT OF FACTS FOR THE APPORTIONMENT OF QUIT OR CROWN RENT.

Heading and Title of Matter.

The Statement of Facts of

SHOWETH—

1. That the lands described in the schedule hereto which form [part of] the ancient denomination of   are charged in the crown Rental with a yearly (quit, crown, composition or otherwise) rent of £ s. d. payable to Her Majesty the Queen under (here

*specify the patent or other instrument creating the rent. If the applica-
tion be for the apportionment of more rents than one, and they are charged
upon different lands, there should be a separate schedule for each, and
the statement should be varied accordingly), and which is in receipt given
[A.B., or if the rent be contributed by two or more persons, the persons
named in the said schedule in the proportions therein specified.
Here add the circumstances (whether under the provisions of a deed
or otherwise) in which the rent is so contributed].*

2. That [parts of] the lands described in the first part of the said
schedule have been sold under the Land Purchase Acts [and it is contemplated selling under the said Acts the residue of such lands, and the
same are the property of the said vendor].

3. That the lands described in the second part of the said schedule
are not the property of the said vendor, and the names and addresses
of the reputed owners thereof are stated therein.

Variation when all the lands are the property of the Vendor.

[3. That the lands described in the second part of the said schedule
are the property of the said vendor, but it is not intended to sell them
under the said Acts.]

4. That no apportionment of the said rent has heretofore been made.

5. That save the proceedings herein, there is not any suit or matter
pending in any Court in relation to the said lands, or to the rents and
profits thereof, and that no person hereinbefore referred to is an infant,
idiot, lunatic, or married woman [or re—*here state the particulars of any
suit or matter, and the names of any persons under disability, giving
the names and addresses as the case may be of the guardian of infant,
committee of lunatic, or husband of married woman.*]

6. That it is expedient that the said rent should be apportioned, and
the proposed apportionment set forth in the said schedule would be just
and fair having regard to the quantities and value of the lands and
the rights of the parties interested.

Schedule referred to in the foregoing Statement.

Townlands, Barony, and County (Ordnance Survey Names only.)	Reference to Map.	Area in Statute Measure of each Town-land or part of a Town-land.	Townparted Valuation, particulars of land and buildings.	Names and Addresses of Owners or reputed Owners	Persons by whom Rents or Chief Rents hereto-fore have been paid and to what proportions.	Proportional Apportionment.	Observations
		A. R. P. £ s. d.				£ s. d.	
		FIRST PART.					
A.—Lands which have been sold.							
B.—Lands which it is contemplated selling.							
		SECOND PART.					
		•					

Affidavit as in Form 18.

FORM 20.

STATEMENT OF FACTS FOR THE APPORTIONMENT OF RENT, FEES, DUTIES OR SERVICES.

Heading and Title of Matter with the following addition :—

And in the matter of the apportionment of a rent of £   s.   d. (or *otherwise as the case may be*) created by an Indenture of [fee-farm grant or lease] dated the   day of   .   18

The Statement of Facts of

SHOWETH—

1. That by the above mentioned Indenture of fee-farm grant (*or lease*) which was made between A. B. of the one part and C. D. of the other part, the said A. B. [in pursuance of the provisions of the Renew-able Leasehold Conversion Act, *or otherwise as the case may be*] granted

(*or devised*) to the said C. D., the lands described in the schedule hereto and in the said indenture described as (*here insert the description of the lands as in the grant or lease*) to hold to the said C. D. and his heirs for ever (*or his executors, administrators, and assigns for the term of, &c.*) subject to the yearly rent of £   s.   d., payable half-yearly as therein mentioned, and to certain conditions, covenants, and agreements on the grantee's (*or lessee's*) part therein contained. (*Here state shortly the particulars of any instrument or circumstances by which the lands were partitioned, or by which any special liability for, or indemnity against any portion of the rent was created, with such statement of the devolution of title as may be necessary to make the statement of facts intelligible to the Commissioner.*)

2. That E. F. of   is the owner of the said rent of £   s. d., and has been in receipt thereof for   years and upwards.

3. That the said   (*i.e. the person making the statement of facts*) has made inquiries to ascertain if there is any superior rent affecting the interest of the said E. F., and to the best of his knowledge, information, and belief, there is no such superior rent (*or otherwise, as the case may be*).

4. That [parts of] the lands described in the first part of the said schedule have been sold under the Land Purchase Acts [and it is contemplated selling under the said Acts the residue of such lands, and the same are the property of the said vendor].

5. That the lands described in the second part of the said schedule are not the property of the said vendor, and the names and addresses of the reputed owners thereof are stated therein.

Variation when all the lands are the property of the vendor.

[5. That the lands described in the second part of the said schedule are the property of the said vendor, but it is not intended to sell them under the said Acts.]

6. That save the proceedings herein there is not any suit or matter pending in any Court in relation to the said rent or lands, and that no person hereinbefore referred to is an infant, idiot, lunatic, or married woman [*save—here state the particulars of any suit or matter, and the names of any persons under disability, giving the names and addresses as the case may be of the guardian of infant, committee of lunatic, or husband of married woman.*]

7. That it is expedient that the said rent should be apportioned, and the proposed apportionment set forth in the said schedule would be just and fair having regard to the quantities and value of the lands, and the rights of the parties interested.

82

SCHEDULE referred to in the foregoing STATEMENT.

Townlands, Barony, and County (Ordnance Survey Names only.)	References to Map.	Area in Statute Measure of each Townland or part of a Townland.	Tenanted Valuation exclusive of buildings.	Names and Addresses of Owners or reputed Owners	Proportion to which the rent has heretofore been paid.	Proposed Apportionment.	Observations.
		A. R. P.	C. s. d.		£ s. d.	£ s. d.	

FIRST PART.

A.—Lands which have been sold.

B.—Lands which it is contemplated selling.

SECOND PART.

Affidavit as in Form 18.

FORM 21.

STATEMENT OF FACTS FOR THE APPORTIONMENT OF A RENT-
CHARGE OR AN ANNUITY.

Heading and Title of Matter, with the following addition :—

And in the matter of the apportionment of a rentcharge (or
annuity) of £   created by a deed dated the   day of
18 .

The Statement of Facts of

SHOWETH—

1. That by the above mentioned deed, dated the
day of   18 , and made between (*here state the
parties to the deed and its nature, whether a marriage settlement or
otherwise.*) A.B. being then seised in fee of the lands described in
the schedule hereto charged the same with an annuity of £

in favour of C.D. (*here specify the particulars of the rentcharge or annuity, whether the same was perpetual, for a term of years, for a life or lives, or by way of jointure, and the particulars of any term of years vested in trustees for securing such rentcharge or annuity. Here also state shortly the particulars of any instrument or circumstances by which the lands were partitioned or by which any special liability for, or indemnity against any portion of the rentcharge or annuity was created, with such statement of the devolution of title as may be necessary to make the statement of facts intelligible to the Commissioner*).

2. That E. F. of   is the owner of and in receipt of the said rentcharge (or annuity).

3. That the [parts of] the lands described in the first part of the said schedule have been sold under the Land Purchase Acts, [and it is contemplated selling under the said Acts the residue of such lands, and the same are the property of the said vendor].

4. That the lands described in the second part of the said schedule are not the property of the said vendor, and the names and addresses of the reputed owners thereof are stated therein.

Variation when all the lands are the property of the vendor.

[4. That the lands described in the second part of the said schedule are the property of the said vendor, but it is not intended to sell them under the said Acts.]

5. That, save the proceedings herein, there is not any suit or matter pending in any court in relation to the said rentcharge (or annuity) or lands, and that no person hereinbefore referred to is an infant, idiot, lunatic, or married woman (save—*here state the particulars of any suit or matter, and the names of any persons under disability, giving the names and addresses as the case may be of the guardian of infant, committee of lunatic, or husband of married woman*).

6. That it is expedient that the said rentcharge (or annuity) should be apportioned, and the proposed apportionment set forth in the said schedule would be just and fair, having regard to the quantities and value of the lands, and the rights of the parties interested.

Schedule referred to in the foregoing Statement.

Townlands, Barony and County (Ordnance Survey names only).	Reference num to Map.	Area in Statute Measure of each Townland or part of a Townland.	Tenement Valuation, exclusive Area of buildings.	Names and Addresses of Owners or reputed Owners.	Proportion in which the Remainder of Annuity has hitherto been paid.	Proposed Apportionment.	Observations.
		A. R. P.	£. s. d.		£. s. d.	£. s. d.	
		FIRST PART.					
A.—Lands which have been sold.							
B.—Lands which it is contemplated selling.							
		SECOND PART.					

Affidavit as in Form 18.

FORM 22.

REQUEST to APPOINT an ARBITRATOR.

Heading and Title of Matter.

Sir,—I hereby require you to appoint an arbitrator to determine the price to be paid for the (*here describe the superior interest, or the apportioned part thereof, as the case may be*), which has been ordered to be redeemed by order made in this matter and dated the   day of   189 , a copy of which is annexed hereto, and all other matters which it appertains to the Court of Arbitration to determine pursuant to the Land Purchase Acts.

And take notice that if for the space of fourteen days from the date of the service of this request upon you, you fail to appoint such arbitrator, I shall apply to the Court to determine the price, as is provided by the said Acts.

Dated this   day of   189 .

(Signed),   E. F.

Here follows a copy of the order for the redemption.

FORM 28.

SUBMISSION TO ARBITRATION AND APPOINTMENT OF ARBITRATORS AND UMPIRE.

Heading and Title of Matter.

Whereas the Irish Land Commission, upon the   day of 189 , made an order in the following terms, viz. :—(*Recite in full the order for redemption.*)

It is hereby agreed by and between A.B., the said vendor, and C. D., the owner (*or tenant for life or otherwise as the case may be*) of the said (*here describe the superior interest*) to refer the determining of the price of the said (*superior interest or apportioned part*) so ordered to be redeemed, to the award of E. F. of   and O. H. of pursuant to the provisions of the Land Purchase Acts. Now the said A. B. hereby appoints the said E. F. to be and act as his arbitrator herein, and the said C. D. hereby appoints the said G. H. to be and act as his arbitrator.

Dated this   day of   189 ,

Signed by the said A. B. in presence of   (Signed),   A. B.

Signed by the said C. D. in presence of   (Signed),   C. D.

The said E. F. and G. H., the arbitrators so hereby appointed, do hereby and before entering upon the matters herein referred to them, in accordance with the provisions of the Land Purchase Acts, appoint L. M. of   to be and act as umpire in case of differences between them.

Dated, &c.

Witness.   (Signed),   E. F.

            (Signed),   G. H.

AWARD.

Heading and Title of Matter.

Whereas the Irish Land Commission, by order, dated the day of 189 , ordered that (*here describe the superior interest or apportional part thereof*) should be redeemed. And whereas *A. B.* and *C. D.*, being unable to agree upon the price to be paid for (*such rent, or otherwise as the case may be*), have referred the determining of the price to be paid to *E. F.* and *G. H.* And by writing under their hands, dated the day of 189 , the said *A. B.* hath appointed *E. F.* to be and act as his arbitrator herein, and the said *C. D.* hath appointed *G. H.* to be and act as his arbitrator herein."

Now, we the said arbitrators, having taken upon ourselves the burden of this reference, and having duly weighed and considered the documentary and other evidence given before us, do hereby publish our award in writing, in manner following, that is to say:—

We award and adjudge that the price to be paid for the said (*rent, or otherwise as the case may be*) is to be the sum of £ . And we do further adjudge and award (*that each party do bear his own costs of the arbitration, and that they do pay in equal proportions our fees and expenses as such arbitrators, or otherwise as the case may be*).

In witness whereof we have hereunto set our hands this day of 189 .

	(Signed),	E. F.
Signed and published in the presence of .	(Signed),	G. H.

UMPIRE's AWARD where ARBITRATORS are unable to agree.

Proceed as before down to.

And whereas the said arbitrators so thereby appointed did, by writing under their hands, dated the day of 189 , before entering into the matter so referred to them, appoint me, *L. M.*, to be and act as umpire in case of difference between them. And whereas the said *E. F.* and *G. H.* have failed to make their award concerning the said price within twenty-one days after the said day of 189 (*or as the case may be*).

Now I, *L. M.*, having taken upon myself the charge of this reference, and having heard, examined, and considered the allegations, witnesses, and evidence of both parties concerning the said price, do make this my award, in writing, of and concerning the said price in manner following, that is to say:—

I award and adjudge, &c. (*as before*).

Form 25.

Allocation Schedule.

Court of the Irish Land Commission.

Land Purchase Acts.

Mr. Commissioner

Record No.

In the Matter of the Estate of   , a Vendor of Land.

Particulars of Fund to be allocated—

Order of Priority.	Date.	Name, Residence, and Addition of Claimant.	Particulars of Demands.	Principal.	Interest or Arrears up to the day of 187	Costs.	Total due for Principal, Interest, and Costs.	Date of Payment.	Ruling of the Commissioner.
				£ s. d.	£ s. d.	£ s. d.	£ s. d.		

Form 26.

Privity for the Lodgment of a Guarantee Deposit.

Heading and Title of Matter.

Name of Tenant Purchaser.	Townland, (Ordnance Survey Name).	Barony.	County.	Amount of Advances.	Amount of Guarantee Deposit.
				£	£

Name of Depositor in full,_____

Postal Address,_____

Occupation or other description,_____

Note.—The above particulars are to be accurately filled in by the Applicant.

Issue receivable order to enable the above-named depositor to lodge the guarantee deposit above-stated, which is to be registered in his name, pursuant to the Rules in that behalf.

Dated this   day of   189

                     Examiner.

Form 37.

NOTICE of MOTION to APPOINT TRUSTEES, for the PURPOSES of the SETTLED LAND ACTS, 1882 to 1890.

COURT of the IRISH LAND COMMISSION.

LAND PURCHASE ACTS.

Record No.

In the Matter of the Estate of A. B.,   a Vendor of Land.

And in the matter of the estate of   situate at   in the county of   settled by a settlement made by an indenture, dated the day of   18 , and made between   [or, by the will of dated   or as the case may be], and in the matter of the Settled Land Acts, 1882 to 1890.

Take notice that counsel will on the   day of   169 , apply to Mr. Justice   on the part of   that O. H. of   and L. J. of   may be appointed trustees under the above mentioned settlement for the purposes of the Settled Land Acts, 1882 to 1890, and that the costs of this application may be directed to be taxed as between solicitor and client, and that the same, when taxed, may be paid out of the property subject to the said settlement, and that for that purpose all necessary directions may be given which application will be grounded on, &c.

Form 38.

STATEMENT of FACTS for the APPOINTMENT of TRUSTEES, under section 66 of the LANDED ESTATES COURT ACT.

COURT OF THE IRISH LAND COMMISSION.

LAND PURCHASE ACTS.

Record No.   .

In the Matter of the Estate of John Brown, a Vendor of Land, and of a Settlement dated the 9th day of May, 1861, executed on the marriage of William Thompson with Jane Moore.

The Statement of facts of Jane Thompson, formerly Moore, showeth as follows :—

By an Indenture bearing date the 9th day of May, 1861, and made between William Thompson of the 1st part ; me, the said Jane Thompson, then Jane Moore, of the 2nd part ; and A. B. and C. D. of the 3rd part, being the settlement executed on the occasion of my marriage with the said Wm. Thompson, it was agreed that a sum of £10,000 should be vested in the said A. B. and C. D., as trustees upon the trusts therein mentioned, and (among others) in trust for the said William Thompson and Jane Moore, successively, during their lives, and after the decease of the survivor, for the children of the said marriage, as therein mentioned.

Pursuant to a power in the said settlement, the said trustees lent £5,000, part of the said trust moneys, to the above mentioned John Brown, on the security of an Indenture of Mortgage, bearing date the 20th day of June, 1863, whereby the said John Brown conveyed certain lands to the said trustees, to secure the said sum of £5,000.

The said mortgaged premises, or part thereof, are the subject of proceedings for sale in this Court, in the Matter of the said Estate, and the said mortgage debt is still a charge upon the said premises.

The other trust funds are a sum of £5,000 *Consols*, now standing in the names of the said *A. B.* and *C. D.*

The said *A. B.* died on the 4th of *July*, 1879, the said *C. D.* was adjudicated a bankrupt on the 7th of *November*, 1882. It is therefore expedient that new trustees of the said settlement should be appointed in place of the said *A. B.* and *C. D.*

E. F. and *G. H.* (*describing them*) are fit and proper persons to be appointed, and they have consented to act as such trustees as by their undertaking dated the   day of   189 , and filed herewith appears; there are no proceedings for the appointment of new trustees of the said settlement pending before any other Court.

The said *William Thompson* died on the 7th day of *March*, 1879. There are three children of the said marriage, *William*, *Sarah*, and *James*, of whom the two latter are infants, aged 19 and 17 respectively, and are now residing with me, the said *Jane Thompson*.

The Applicant submits that the said *C. D.* should be removed from being such trustee as aforesaid, and that new trustees should be appointed of the said settlement and trust funds by an Order of the Court, and that provision should be made for the payment out of the said trust fund, by such trustees when appointed, of the costs of this statement, the order to be made thereon, and the proper and necessary proceedings thereunder.

     Dated this   day of   189 .

          (Signed),   *Jane Thompson.*

I, the said *Jane Thompson*, make oath and say that I have read the foregoing statement, and that the same is true to the best of my knowledge, information, and belief, and that I am entitled to the relief sought.

             Sworn, &c.

Form 29.

Notice of Lodgment of Surveyor's Report and Scheme for Partition.

Heading and Title of matter.

Take Notice that in pursuance of the order in this matter, dated the   day of   189 , Mr.   the surveyor thereby appointed, has lodged in the Registrar's Office of the Irish Land Commission, 24, Upper Merrion-street, Dublin, his report and map with scheme for partition of   the lands of   , situate in the Barony of   , and County of   , and held   , and further Take Notice that any person interested in said partition, is at liberty to inspect the said report, map, and scheme, and that if no application be made to the Commissioner within fourteen days after the service of this notice to vary or amend the said report and scheme for partition the same shall stand confirmed, and a Final Order for Partition will be made in accordance with such report, map, and scheme.

         Dated   day of   189 .

   To

              Solicitor for

Form 30.

Commission to Examine Witnesses.

Heading and Title of Matter.

Victoria by the Grace of God of the United Kingdom of Great Britain and Ireland Queen Defender of the Faith and soforth to [state name and address of examiner or commissioner appointed] greeting.

We hereby authorise you upon the   day of
189 , at   , in the presence of the solicitors for the persons appearing in this matter, or in the presence of their or of any of their lawfully appointed substitutes, or otherwise notwithstanding the absence of any of them, to swear the witnesses who shall be produced for examination in the said matter, and cause them to be examined, and their depositions to be reduced into writing. We further authorise you to adjourn (if necessary) the said examinations from time to time and from place to place, as you may find expedient. And We command you upon the examinations being completed, to transmit the depositions and the whole proceedings had and done before you, together with this commission to the Registrar of the said Court.

Witness the seal of the Irish Land Commission the
day of   189 .

Registrar,

Taken out by

Form 31.

Summons for the Attendance of Witnesses and for the Production of Documents.

Heading and Title of Matter.

You and each of you are hereby required to attend before Mr. Commissioner   , at his Court [or Chamber] at 24, Upper Merrion-street, Dublin, at the hour of   o'clock on   day the day of   189 , and from day to day there to be examined in relation to this matter (a). And herein fail not at your peril.

Dated this   day of   189 ,

To
        of

Registrar.

. (a). In a summons for the production of documents here add "and " you are also hereby required to produce to the Court all papers, docu- " ments, letters, writings, and other evidences in your power, possession, " or procurement, relating to this matter," [or otherwise as the case may be.]

Form 32.

Writ of Sequestration.

Heading and Title of Matter.

Victoria by the Grace of God of the United Kingdom of Great Britain and Ireland Queen Defender of the Faith and soforth to [*name and address of sequestrator*] greeting.

Whereas by an Order made in this matter and dated the day of   189 , it was ordered that *A.B.* should [pay into the Bank of Ireland to the credit of this matter the sum of £   or as the case may be]. Know you therefore that We in confidence of your prudence and fidelity, have given, and by these presents do give to you full power and authority to enter upon all the messuages, lands, tenements and real estate whatsoever of the said *A.B.*, and to collect, receive, and sequester into your hands not only all the rents and profits of his said messuages, lands, tenements and real estate, but also all his goods, chattels and personal estates whatsoever; and therefore We command you, that you do at certain proper and convenient days and hours, go to and enter upon all the messuages, lands, tenements, and real estates of the said *A.B.*, and that you do collect, take, and get into your hands not only the rents and the profits of his said real estate, but also all his goods, chattels and personal estate, and detain and keep the same under sequestration in your hands until the said *A. B.* shall [pay into Court to the credit of this matter the said sum of £   , or as the case may be, and] clear his contempt, and this Court make other order to the contrary.

Witness the seal of the Irish Land Commission the day of   189 ,

Registrar.

Form 33.

Requisition to have the Order of a Commissioner not made upon a Question of Law reconsidered by a Judicial Commissioner and two other Commissioners.

Heading and Title of Matter.

I am aggrieved by the order of Mr. Commissioner   , made in this matter and dated the   day of   189 , whereby it was ordered   and I require to have the said order reconsidered by a Judicial Commissioner and two other Commissioners; and I certify that the question involved is not one of law.

Dated this   day of   189 .

Solicitor for

APPLICATION BY A TENANT FOR AN ADVANCE TO ENABLE HIM TO PURCHASE HIS HOLDING FROM THE LAND JUDGE.

COURT OF THE IRISH LAND COMMISSION.

LAND PURCHASE ACTS.

Record No. A——.

In the Matter of the Estate of
Owner;

Ex parte

Petitioner.

I, the Tenant
in occupation of the holding
described in the first part of the
Schedule hereto, *have been declared
the purchaser of the Lands in the*
said Schedule described for the sum of £ [or] *intend to offer the
sum of £ for the Lands in the said Schedule described.*

The said lands have been [or] *my offer will be conditional on the said
lands being sold to me in fee-simple discharged* from all superior
interests, save (a) and I hereby apply to the Irish Land Commission to advance to me, pursuant to the said Acts, the sum of £
Guaranteed Land Stock, for the purpose of such purchase, which advance
is to be repaid as is by the said Acts provided.

(a) Here insert the particulars of any superior interests which the sale is made subject to.

SCHEDULE.

[*Same as that to Form 10.*]

Signed by the said Tenant in presence of—	Dated this day of 189 .
Name,	Signature of Tenant,
Address,	Postal Address,
Occupation,	Occupation or Description,

[*Here follows the Affidavit as in Form 10, changing the word "Agreement"
to "Application" in Paragraph 5 and in the Jurat.*]

DIRECTIONS AS TO PREPARATION OF APPLICATION AND AFFIDAVIT.

The Application and Affidavit must be neatly and accurately prepared, without any blanks, and must correspond with the Court rental,
otherwise the application cannot be received.

When the Tenant is a female she should be described either as
"spinster," "widow," or "wife of A.B."

In filling up the column headed "Tenure of Tenant," state whether
the Tenant holds under Fee-farm Grant (giving date and parties), under
Lease or agreement in writing (giving date, parties, and term), under a
tenancy from year to year, or how otherwise. If the rent be a Judicial
one, state on what date and how it is fixed.

UNDERTAKING BY TENANT TO PURCHASE HIS HOLDING FROM THE
LAND COMMISSION, AND APPLICATION FOR ADVANCE.

COURT OF THE IRISH LAND COMMISSION.

LAND PURCHASE ACTS.

Record No. A.——

* In the Matter of the Estate of   I   the
                    Owner;   } Tenant in occupation of the hold-
   Ex parte   Petitioner. } ing described in the first part of
the Schedule hereto, hereby propose and undertake as follows:—

1. In case the said Commission buy the Lands described in the said
Schedule, I will purchase the same from them in fee-simple——

——————————————————————————

at the price of £——, to be paid as follows:—

*By an Advance to be made by the said Commission to me, of
£——, Guaranteed Land Stock.*

By a Cash payment by me to the said Commission, of £——.

2. The Lodgment of this undertaking with the Irish Land Commission
is to be deemed an application by me for an advance pursuant to the
said Acts, to be repaid as is by the said Acts provided.

SCHEDULE.

[*Same as that to Form 10.*]

Signed by the said Tenant in } presence of—	Dated this day of 189 .
Name,_____	Signature of Tenant,_____
Address,_____	Postal Address,_____
Occupation,_____	Occupation or Description,_____

[*Here follows the Affidavit as in Form* 10, *changing the word "Agreement" to "Undertaking" in Paragraph* 5, *and in the Jurat.*]

N.B.—If the Estate is not being sold in the Land Judges Court, the Title of the Matter should
be;—In the Matter of the Estate of   a Vendor of Land.

DIRECTIONS AS TO PREPARATION OF UNDERTAKING AND AFFIDAVIT.

The Undertaking and Affidavit must be neatly and accurately prepared, without any blanks, and all clauses not applicable to the case must be struck out, otherwise the Undertaking cannot be received.

When the Tenant is a female she should be described either as "spinster," "widow," or "wife of A.B."

CLAUSE 1.—When it is proposed to purchase additional land under the "Purchase of Land (Ireland) Amendment Act, 1889," insert after "superior interests," "together with the additional land specified in the second part of the said schedule." Here also insert any rights of grazing, or turbary, or other rights which are appurtenant to the holding, and which are exercised over lands not included therein, e.g., "together with such right of grazing and cutting turf as has heretofore been exercised by the said Tenant upon the bog on the lands of Blackacre, in the possession of   , containing   statute measure or thereabouts." Here insert also the particulars of any superior interests which the purchaser proposes, the sale shall be made subject to.

FORM 36.

APPLICATION BY A LANDLORD TO THE LAND COMMISSION TO PURCHASE HIS ESTATE FOR RE-SALE.

Heading and Title of Matter.

I the above named Vendor propose to sell to the Irish Land Commission for the sum of £   guaranteed land stock, the lands comprised in the originating statement filed by me on the   day of   189 , and I hereby apply to the Irish Land Commission to purchase the same for re-sale to the tenants thereof, and I undertake to pay to the Irish Land Commission the reasonable expenses incurred by them in connexion with the said Sale.

Dated this   day of   189 .

Signature of Vendor _____

N.B.—This Application must be accompanied by undertakings in Form 35 from the requisite number of tenants to buy their holdings. The Land Commission cannot buy an estate unless at least four-fifths in number and value of the tenants are prepared to buy their holdings.

FORM 37.

ORIGINATING NOTICE UNDER THE REDEMPTION OF RENT (IRELAND)
ACT, 1891.

County_____

No. _____

COURT OF THE IRISH LAND COMMISSION.

REDEMPTION OF RENT (IRELAND) ACT, 1891.

Name of (*)_____, and Residence, { _____ } (a) "Lessor" or "Grantor."
if known.

Name and Residence of the above { _____ }
person's Agent, if any.

Name and Residence of (*)_____ { _____ } (b) "Lessee" or "Grantee."

Post Office from which he receives } _____
his letters.

DESCRIPTION OF HOLDING.

County_____	Barony_____			Electoral Division_____					
Ordnance Survey Names of Townlands (each on a separate line).	Area, Statute Measure, of the portion of each Townland.			Rent of Holding.			Gross Poor Law Valuation.		
	A.	R.	P.	£	s.	d.	£	s.	d.

ORIGINATING NOTICE OF APPLICATION BY A (*)_____ TO
REDEEM HIS RENT OR IN THE ALTERNATIVE TO FIX A FAIR RENT.

I,_____, the (*)_____, being in bona fide (b) "Lessee" or "Grantee."
occupation of the above holding, which is held under a (*)_____ dated (c) "Lease" or "Fee-farm Grant."
the_____day of_____, 18___, and made between (*) (d) State summarily the parties, and in the case of a Lease, the term.
_____
at the yearly rent of £_____, apply to the Court for an Order for the
redemption of the said rent, or, in the alternative, for an Order fixing
the Fair Rent to be hereafter paid for the said holding.

Dated this_____day of_____189___

Signature,_____

Occupation or Description,_____

To the (*)_____ (a) "Lessor" or "Grantor."

Name of Solicitor for the (*)_____ (b) "Lessee" or "Grantee."

Registered Place of Business,_____

FORM 38.

CONSENT TO REDEMPTION UNDER THE REDEMPTION OF RENT (IRELAND) ACT, 1891.

COURT OF THE IRISH LAND COMMISSION.

LAND PURCHASE ACTS.

In the Matter of the Estate of

A Vendor of land.

I the above named Vendor do hereby consent as follows, viz. :—

1. That the Court do make an order pursuant to the provisions of the Redemption of Rent (Ireland) Act, 1891, for the redemption of the rent specified in the Schedule hereto, payable to me out of the holding therein described, by , the (a) named in the Originating Notice dated the day of 189 , which has been served on me.

(a) "Lessee" or "Grantee".

2. That such redemption be carried into effect by means of a vesting order under the provisions of the Land Purchase Acts, vesting the said holding in the said (a) in fee-simple, freed and discharged from all superior interests as defined by section 31 of the Land Law (Ireland) Act, 1896, and from all other charges and incumbrances.

3. That interest upon the redemption price of the said rent at the rate of four per cent. per annum shall be payable in lieu of the rent from the date hereof until such redemption price shall be paid into Court.

Provided that if the said (a) be not entitled to apply to redeem the said rent under the provisions of the Redemption of Rent (Ireland) Act, 1891, this consent shall be void.

SCHEDULE.

County _____ Barony _____ Electoral Division _____

Reference to Map (to be filled in by Land Commission).	Ordnance Survey names of Townlands (each on a separate line).	Area Statute Measure of the portion of each Townland to be sold.			Tenement Valuation.	Rent paid by Tenant.			Tenure of Tenant, i.e. under Purchase Grant giving date and parties; or under Lease giving date, parties, and term.
		a.	r.	p.	£ s. d.	£	s.	d.	

Signed by the Vendor in presence of \ Dated this day of 189 .

Name,_____ | Signature of Vendor,_____

Address,_____ | Postal Address,_____

Occupation,_____ / Occupation or Description,_____

Name of Solicitor for Vendor,_____

Registered place of business,_____

FORM 39.

NOTICE OF LODGMENT OF CONSENT TO REDEMPTION.

COURT OF THE IRISH LAND COMMISSION.

LAND PURCHASE ACTS.

In the Matter of the Estate of

A Vendor of land.

SIR,

Take notice that I have this day lodged in the Irish Land Commission a consent to the making of an order for redemption in pursuance of your Originating Notice, dated the   day of   , 189 .

Solicitor for the said Vendor.

To

FORM 40.

APPLICATION FOR AN ADVANCE UNDER THE REDEMPTION OF RENT (IRELAND) ACT, 1891.

COURT OF THE IRISH LAND COMMISSION.
LAND PURCHASE ACTS.

In the Matter of the Estate of

a Vendor of land.

Name of Tenant,_____

DESCRIPTION OF HOLDING.

County_____	Barony_____		Electoral Division_____		
Reference to Map.	Ordnance Survey names of Townlands (such as a separate item).	Area Statute Measure of the portion of each Townland to be sold.	Tenement Valuation.	Rent paid by Tenant.	Tenure of Tenant, f.e., under Fee-farm Grant, giving date and parties; or under Lease giving date, parties, and term.
		A. R. P.	£ s. d.	£ s. d.	

Date of conditional order for redemption, the   day of   189 .

Amount of Redemption price, £

Amount of Advance required, £

Amount to be paid in cash by Tenant, £

I,_____the before named Tenant, make oath and say, as follows :

1. That the foregoing particulars of the holding are true, to the best of my knowledge and belief.

G

(a) For-farm Grant or Lease.

2. I reside on and have been in the occupation of the said holding and paying the rent therefor since the Year 18 , and I hold the same as Tenant, as in the said Schedule is stated (and the said (*) _____ is still not, note in my* possession).

* still not, note in whose possession.

3. There is not any person in occupation of the said holding as Tenant or otherwise save as mentioned in the following Schedule :—

If there are no under-tenants fill in the word "none" where marked * * *

Names of the Persons in occupation or under-tenants or otherwise.	Area in Statute Measure.			Rent (if any) payable by each occupier.			When payable.	Terms or estate of occupancy.
	A.	R.	P.	£	s.	d.		
* * *								

4. There is not any charge or incumbrance affecting my interest in the said holding save those specified in the following Schedule :—

Schedule containing particulars of Mortgages, Charges created by deposit of Lease or otherwise, or Charges in favour of the Commissioners of Public Works in Ireland affecting the Tenant's Interest in the Holding.

If there are no incumbrances, fill in the word "none" where marked † † †

Date.	Name and Address of Incumbrancer.	Particulars of Incumbrance, Mortgage, or otherwise.	Principal Sum due.		
			£	s.	d.
* * *					
			£.		

5. I hereby apply to the Irish Land Commission for an advance pursuant to the Land Purchase Acts of the sum specified above, the same to be repaid as is by the said Acts provided.

* If the Tenant has previously applied for any advance write "save an advance of £ for" giving the particulars.

6. I have not obtained from or (except by this Application) applied to the Irish Land Commission for an advance of any sum for the purchase of any land.* _____

† If the deponent be illiterate have insert "his to." The words in Italics may be struck out unless the deponent be a marksman.

SWORN before me this _____ day of _____ 189__
at _____
in the County of _____ and I know the Deponent, the whole of the foregoing application and affidavit having been first read over by†——the Deponent who appeared perfectly to understand the same, and made h—— mark thereto in my presence.

Form 41.

Notice of Conditional Order for Redemption under the Redemption of Rent (Ireland) Act, 1891.

Court of the Irish Land Commission.

Land Purchase Acts.

Record No.

In the Matter of the Estate of

A Vendor of land.

Sir,

Take notice that on the   day of   189   , an Originating Statement was filed on behalf of the said Vendor affecting part of the Lands of   situate in the Barony of   and County of   , and containing   acres   roods and   perches statute measure or thereabouts, in the occupation of   as Tenant to the said Vendor under   dated the   day of 18   ,   at the yearly rent of £   ; and that the Court has by order dated the   day of   189   , conditionally ordered the redemption of the said rent at the price of £   , and such redemption will be carried into effect by means of a vesting order under the provisions of the Land Purchase Acts vesting the said lands in the said tenant in fee-simple, freed and discharged from all superior interests as defined by section 31 of the Land Law (Ireland) Act, 1896, and from all other charges and incumbrances.

Your name appearing in the said Originating Statement as being entitled to [here state the nature of the superior interest, charge, incumbrance, or other estate or interest to which the person is entitled], this notice is given to enable you to make any application to the Court that you may be advised in the event of such redemption being prejudicial to your rights.

And further take notice that if no application to the contrary be made by you, by motion to the Commissioner upon notice to me, within fourteen days from the date of the service of this notice upon you, the redemption will be completed in due course without further notice to you.

Dated this   day of   189   .

Solicitor for the Vendor.

[Registered address.]

To

Form 42.

Certificate to Register Apprentice or Clerk.

Court of the Irish Land Commission.

I hereby certify that Mr. (a)   is exclusively employed by me as (a) Name in full.
my (b)   and that he is a fit and competent person to transact my (b) "Apprentice or Clerk."
business in this Court; and I undertake to be responsible for his acts in
the ordinary transaction of my business in the said Court. And I further

O 2

undertake to be responsible for his receipts for deeds and other
documents, and for the safe custody and return of all deeds and documents obtained by him on my behalf.

Dated this   day of   189 .

Solicitor.

Address

Witness

FORM 43.

CERTIFICATE OF REGISTRATION OF APPRENTICE OR CLERK.

COURT OF THE IRISH LAND COMMISSION.

day of   189

I certify that Mr.   is the registered [apprentice or clerk] of
Mr.   Solicitor, of No.   street.

Keeper of Records.

FORM 44.

WRIT OF FIERI FACIAS FOR COSTS.

Heading and Title of Matter.

Victoria, by the Grace of God, of the United Kingdom of Great
Britain and Ireland, Queen, Defender of the Faith and soforth, to the
Sheriff of the County of   greeting :—

We command you that, of the goods and chattels of
in your Bailiwick, you cause to be made the sum of
and also interest thereon at the rate of £4 per cent. per annum from
the   day of   189 , which by order of our Court
of the Irish Land Commission, dated the   day of
189 , was adjudged to be paid by the said
to   for costs in the said Order mentioned. And
that you do cause the said money and interest to be paid to the
said   in pursuance of the said Order, and do
make a return to the said Court of the manner in which you shall
have executed this Writ immediately after the execution thereof.

Dated this   day of   189 .

Registrar.

Levy £   and also interest thereon at £4 per cent. per annum from
the   day of   189 , besides Sheriff's poundage, fees, and
expenses of execution, together with the sum of 10s. 6d. for the costs
of this Writ.

This Writ was issued by   of
Solicitor for the said

Form 45.

Affidavit to Ground Application for Order for Possession.

Court of the Irish Land Commission.

Land Purchase Acts.

In the Matter of the Holding of , in the Lands of
Barony County sold by the Irish Land Commission.
I of make oath and say as follows :—

1. That on the day of last, I purchased from the Irish
Land Commission that part of the lands of containing statute
measure or thereabouts, situate in the barony of and county of

2. That on the day of last, the Irish Land Commission
executed a conveyance to me of the said lands (or by order vested the
said lands in me and that such conveyance (or vesting order) was not
made subject to any tenancies.

3. That on the day of last, I demanded from E.F., whom
I found in occupation of the said lands, the possession thereof, and he
refused to give me such possession.

4. That at the time of making such demand I produced to the said
E.F., a certificate under the hand of the Solicitor to the Irish Land
Commission of my purchase and my title to the possession of the said
lands.

Sworn, &c.

Form 46.

Order to Sheriff to put Purchaser into Possession.

Heading and Title as in Form 45.

Upon motion of solicitor for C. D., the purchaser in this matter, and
on reading the conveyance by the Irish Land Commission to the said
C. D., dated the day of 189 (or the order dated
the day of 189 , vesting in the said C.D.) that part of the
lands of containing statute measure or thereabouts, situate
in the barony of and county of and the affidavit of the said
C. D., filed the day of 169 .

It is ordered by the Court that the sheriff of the county of do,
and he is hereby required and commanded immediately after sight or
receipt hereof, to go to the said part of the lands of situate as
aforesaid, and without delay to give or cause to be given to the said
C. D., or his assigns, the full, quiet, and peaceable possession of the
said part of the said lands, with all and singular the appurtenances, [save
and except the respective parts and portions of the said lands and here-
ditaments now or lately in the possession of, &c.].

Dated this day of 189 .

Registrar.

Directions as to the Preparation of Abstracts of Title.

The Ordnance Survey names of the lands to which title is being shown should be set forth at the head of the abstract, and if title is being shown to a portion only of any townland, the area in statute measure of such portion should be set out.

The date of every instrument abstracted, and of the registration or enrolment thereof should be stated in the margin: if the instrument has not been registered, a statement to that effect should appear in the margin. In the case of a will, the date of the document itself and of the granting of probate, and of the testator's death, should appear in like manner. It should also be stated whether the original instrument abstracted or a copy is lodged, and if the original be not lodged its absence should be accounted for. If neither the original nor a copy be forthcoming there should be a reference to the evidence from which the abstract was prepared.

The abstract should commence with the root of title. If the land is held in fee under a Crown grant, and unless the root of title be a conveyance by the Incumbered Estates Court, Landed Estates Court, or Land Judges, or a declaration of title, an extract from the patent should be given, showing that there is no reversion in the Crown, that the lands are held in fee, and whether they are subject to quit or crown rent. If the lands are held under lease the lease should be abstracted. It will not be necessary to state all the intermediate steps down to the date of the abstract. As a general rule it will be sufficient to derive title from some person absolutely entitled to the fee or to a lease about forty years prior. Every instrument relating to the title should be abstracted: even mortgages which have been paid off, the lands being reconveyed, should be shortly noticed. An abstract ought to be a careful abridgment, not a mere copy of the instrument or of any part thereof. Conciseness may be obtained by avoiding the introduction of unnecessary or duplicate words to express the same idea, and by combining the abstract of common clauses to a mere reference to them: thus such language as—"a certain bond or obligation," "upon, to, and for," ought not to be used in an abstract, and is likely to lead to a ruling whereby a considerably less sum may be allowed as costs than would be allowed in the case of an abstract of equal length properly drawn. The names and descriptions of the parcels in a deed should be accurately set out; but if they are afterwards granted in any other deed by the same names and descriptions it will be sufficient in abstracting such other deeds to state that they are conveyed by the same names and descriptions as in the former deed: or, if the variance is very slight, it will be sufficient to show what the variance is. The same remark is applicable to wills. The common clauses in a deed, such as covenants for title, for quiet enjoyment, for further assurance, and against incumbrances for indemnity of trustees, payment of rent, cesser of terms, &c., should be referred to as briefly as possible: *the contracts, consideration, and habendum should be more fully abstracted, and so should the limitations as far as may be necessary*: that is to say, if a limitation has taken effect, whereby it has become impossible that the subsequent limitations can take effect, the latter should not be abstracted, e.g., if any tenant in tail has after coming into possession executed a disentailing deed duly enrolled, the subsequent limitations should be omitted from the abstract. Recitals of deeds previously abstracted or recited should be referred to thus—"And reciting the deed of 14th July, 1847, abstracted (or recited), page 6." At the end of every deed it should be stated by what parties it has been executed, and with what solemnities (if any): and if it has been enrolled, or acknowledged by a married woman, or the acknowledgment certified, such facts, with the dates thereof, should be stated. If the instrument abstracted is a marriage settlement it should be immediately followed by a statement of the issue of the marriage, and of the dates of their respective births, and of the deaths of such of them as are dead. When an estate is transferred by the death of any person, the date of his death should be stated, and the date of the death of any person having powers of charging should be stated. When a person takes as heir, it is not enough to state that he is heir; it must be shewn how he is heir by setting out so much of the pedigree as proves it. Births, deaths, and the facts of pedigree, when stated should be accompanied by a reference to the evidence by which such facts are proved.

In every abstract the deduction of title to the lands should be carried on continuously from its commencement to its completion, and should not as a general rule be interrupted by introducing the deduction of title to charges or incumbrances, especially if such charges are still existing, or any other collateral matter. The title to such charges or incumbrances, if necessary, and the instruments dealing with them, should be set forth in a separate part of the abstract, with a proper heading for each charge or incumbrance; and a reference to the page of such devolution of title to the incumbrance should be made when the creation of the incumbrance is stated in its proper place.

When an abstract of title has been prepared for any purpose other than a sale in the Land Commission, it should be produced to the Examiner together with such evidence if any as may be necessary to show the purpose for which it was prepared, and his directions taken as to whether the title may merely be continued from the close of such abstract or how far it may be utilised. Such abstract, if used for the purpose of a sale or mortgage effected not less than twelve years prior to the proceedings, may by permission of an Examiner, to be given in writing in the fold thereof, be lodged without a verifying affidavit, but on the reading the Examiner may, if he deem it necessary, direct the same to be verified.

DIRECTIONS AS TO THE PREPARATION OF AFFIDAVITS UNDER
ORDER XX., RULE 16.

The title must be set out in the affidavit in as concise a manner as is possible, consistently with clearness. The effect of deeds, wills, and other documents should, as a rule, be given instead of an abstract in detail of their contents.

The affidavit must state in what manner it is proposed that the price or compensation shall be paid or applied. If the superior interest redeemed be subject to a quit or Crown rent, a matter which can in the case of a fee-farm or other rent, be ascertained by an inspection of the schedule of incumbrances, such rent would generally be a first charge on the price or compensation, and should therefore be redeemed thereout. If the superior interest redeemed be an impropriate tithe rent-charge, a certificate from the Quit Rent Office showing whether the same be subject to a quit or Crown rent, must accompany the affidavit.

If such superior interest be subject to incumbrances, and it be proposed to apply the price, or compensation, in satisfaction or reduction of an incumbrance, the affidavit should not as a rule set forth the title subsequent to the instrument creating the incumbrance, save so far as may be necessary in order to show in whom such incumbrance is vested; but it should state the name or names of the person or persons entitled to the superior interest subject to incumbrances, and refer to the instrument under which he or they is or are so entitled.

If it be proposed to pay the price or compensation to trustees the affidavit should show that they are entitled to receive the same as being trustees with a power of sale, or trustees for the purposes of the Settled Land Acts or otherwise as the case may be.

If it be proposed to pay such price or compensation or part thereof to a person or persons beneficially entitled, the affidavit must, unless the Commissioner otherwise directs, be made by such person or persons, and must contain a statement to the effect that the deponent has not charged, incumbered, or dealt with his estate in such superior interest, or the price or compensation representing the same save as appears by the affidavit.

SCHEDULE OF FEES.

PART I.

	£	s.	d.
ABSTRACT :			
Drawing draft abstract, so far as the Examiner shall certify his approbation thereof, for every six folios, or fractional part thereof, ...	0	4	0
ADVERTISEMENT :			
Draft advertisement, ...	0	8	8
Or, at option of Solicitor, per folio, . .	0	0	8
AFFIDAVIT :			
Draft affidavit. For the first six folios, or under, .	0	4	0
For each additional folio, . . .	0	0	8
For marking each exhibit, . . .	0	0	6

When an affidavit is annexed to a document merely to verify or identify it, the entire is to be considered as one document, and no separate fees are to be allowed for attendance, draft, engrossment, copy, or signature.

AGREEMENTS FOR PURCHASE : Applications and undertakings under Forms 34, 35, 38, and 40.

Solicitor's fee for preparing and completing agreement for each sale on an estate, provided six months have elapsed since the completion of the previous sale, including all scrivenery, and printing, fees, attendances, and other business incident to the preparation, lodgment and verification of same, but exclusive of the expenses of maps and other necessary expenditure.

	£	s.	d.
For one such agreement or undertaking, the purchase money being under £500, . . .	1	0	0
For one such agreement when the purchase money exceeds £500, ...	2	0	0
For more than one and not exceeding five such agreements in the same estate, . . .	3	0	0
For each subsequent agreement after five, not exceeding 10, ...	0	10	0
For each subsequent agreement after ten, not exceeding 100, ...	0	6	0
For each subsequent agreement after 100, . .	0	4	0
ALLOCATION SCHEDULE :			
For preparing Allocation Schedule, for each item, except costs of sale, . . .	0	5	0

AMENDMENTS :

No charge to be allowed for any amendment in an Originating Statement, Abstract of Title, or other document lodged in Court by a Solicitor, unless specially allowed.

	£	s.	d.

APPEARANCES:
Entering an appearance and all attendances in relation to same, — 0 0 8

APPOINTMENT OF TRUSTEES:
Instructions and perusals, — 0 13 4
For all business done up to and including the taking out of the order when Counsel employed, — 6 6 0
When Counsel not employed, — 4 4 0
(Counsel not to be allowed unless certified for.)

APPORTIONMENT OF TITHE RENTCHARGE:
Fee for preparing and lodging form of application for apportionment of Tithe rentcharge payable to the Land Commission (Forms Nos. 16 and 17), including calculations of apportionments, scrivenery, instructions and correspondence, — 0 10 0
Or at the option of the Solicitor, per folio, — 0 1 0

ATTENDANCES:
Attending on Client, or any person by his direction, not exceeding one hour, — 0 6 8
For each subsequent hour, — 0 6 8
Not to exceed in one day, — 1 0 0
For each day Cause or Motion in Day List and not at hearing, — 0 6 8
Each day it is at hearing, — 0 13 4
Not to exceed in one day, — 1 0 0
(A fee of 13s. 4d. is allowed on motions where an order is made up by the Registrar or pronounced by the Court.)
Not to be allowed unless a competent person attends acquainted with the facts and proceedings in the cause, and having the proper documents in readiness.
Attending on each witness taking evidence, — 0 6 8
Attending Counsel with Brief, Case, or other instructions, — 0 6 8
And where two or more Counsel employed, — 0 13 4
Attending to settle and afterwards to read over the engrossment of an affidavit, but only one fee, — 0 6 8
To be increased according to circumstances, but never to exceed in town, — 1 6 8
Each newspaper in which an advertisement is inserted exclusive of charges by proprietors of newspapers, — 0 2 4
Attending printer to have notice or other document other than agreement printed, — 0 6 8
Attending to procure Accountant's Account or certificate of funds, — 0 3 4
Attending for certificate of deeds lodged, — 0 3 4
Attending for certificate of appearances, objections or claims lodged, each, — 0 3 4
To be increased according to circumstances, each to, — 0 6 8
Certificate of lodgment of Abstract of Title, — 0 3 4
Attending checking and examining map, — 0 6 8
Attending Examiner to settle and sign advertisements 0 6 8

	£	s.	d.

ATTENDANCES :—*continued.*

Attending consultation of Counsel, .   .   . | 0 | 6 | 8

Attending to obtain consent to act as Guardian *ad litem,* or next friend, .   .   . | 0 | 6 | 8

Attending to procure consent to be signed by another Solicitor, .   .   . | 0 | 6 | 8

If to be signed by two, .   .   . | 0 | 13 | 4

If by a greater number, but never to exceed, . | 1 | 0 | 0

Attendance to vouch publication of notice to claimants, | 0 | 3 | 4

Attending to bespeak all necessary documents, . | 0 | 6 | 8

Like to file same, ... | 0 | 6 | 8

If several affidavits or other document ought to be filed or bespoken at one time from one officer, the Taxing Officer is to exercise his discretion to increase this charge, but never to allow more than | 1 | 0 | 0

Attending on Taxation of costs, each Solicitor whose costs are under taxation, and for the Solicitor or Solicitors opposing the taxation, for each 100 items or fractional part thereof, | 0 | 6 | 8

For all attendances to lodge money in Bank, including the procuring of the privity, | 0 | 13 | 4

Attendance of Solicitor from his house for each day that he shall be necessarily absent, exclusive of all carriage expenses, but to include living, . | 3 | 3 | 0

Attendance of Solicitor in the country when he shall return the same day, provided such distance from Dublin shall exceed twelve miles, to include living, but not carriage expenses, .   . | 3 | 3 | 0

> If twelve miles or less at the discretion of the Taxing Officer.

Attendance of a clerk in the country (when necessary), including all expenses except carriage hire, for each day, .   .   . | 1 | 10 | 0

> Where a Solicitor shall be required to leave Ireland, whether to London or elsewhere, his travelling expenses shall be allowed according to the distance and convenience of travelling, and to the reasonable rate of expense which such Solicitor might incur in the same journey if solely engaged in his private affairs.

Attendance at Valuation Office to bespeak Ordnance Map and Certificate of Valuation, .   . | 0 | 6 | 8

Attending to register or enrol any deed or order, and for all duties relating thereto, including the returning of the deed or order, and the counting of same and memorial, and drawing and signing certificate and affidavit, | 1 | 0 | 0

Attending tenants or Solicitor for tenants for copy lease agreement or proposal where necessary, | 0 | 6 | 8

> If the document be obtained through a Solicitor, such Solicitor to be entitled to a fee of 6s. 8d. for attendance therewith.

Attending Registrar bespeaking and for order, . | 0 | 6 | 8

	£	s.	d.

CERTIFYING:

Certifying any deed, instrument, or writing when required by the Court,   0   3   6

COMMISSIONER OF OATHS:

Commissioner's fee for affidavit for each deponent,   0   1   6

    „   „   marking each exhibit,   0   0   6

                  Not exceeding in all,   2   0   0

CONSENTS:

Drawing and signing consent, undertaking, or admission,   0   5   0

Or at option of the Solicitor, per folio,   0   0   6

CONSENT TO REDEEM UNDER REDEMPTION OF RENT ACT (FORM 38):

Fee for preparing, completing, and lodging consent to redemption under Redemption of Rent Act, 1891,   1   0   0

CONVEYANCING:

For drawing any deed, final order for partition, apportionment, memorial, or other instrument, per folio,   0   2   0

Where the draft exceeds 100 folios, the excess to be allowed at per folio,   0   1   0

Engrossing, per folio,   0   0   6

COPIES:

All copies of documents not herein provided for, each folio,   0   0   3

Engrossing Abstracts of Title for the Examiner, for every six folios or under,   0   2   0

And for every additional six folios or fractional part thereof,   0   2   0

Copy thereof for use, per folio,   0   0   4

Engrossing affidavit, or statement of facts, for every six folios or under,   0   2   0

And for each additional folio or fractional part thereof,   0   0   4

Copy of all advertisements,   0   1   0

Or at the option of the Solicitor, per folio,   0   0   3

Copy Schedule of deeds, per page of twenty-eight lines,   0   1   6

For engrossment on parchment, Requisition for Registrar of Deeds, five folios or under,   0   5   0

If more than five, for each additional folio,   0   1   0

All necessary copies of such searches, for four office sheets and under,   0   1   0

For each subsequent folio,   0   0   3

COPIES:

Copy of all notices, for each copy, including postage stamp and envelope directed,   0   1   0

Copy Brief or Case for Counsel, for six folios or under,   0   2   0

And for six folios or fractional part thereof,   0   2   0

Copy costs, per item,   0   0   1

COSTS:

Drawing costs for taxation, per item,   0   0   1

Perusing costs for opposition on taxation, for each 100 items, or fractional part thereof,   0   3   4

Attending taxation of costs, for each 100 items, or fractional part thereof,   0   6   8

	£	s.	d.

DRAFTS :

In computing the length of all documents used in this Court the folio to consist of 72 words.

Draft brief for counsel, for every 6 folios or fractional part thereof, ... | 0 | 3 | 4 |

No perusals of any kind to be allowed preparatory to drawing pleadings, deeds, or other documents, either between party and party, or between Solicitor and Client.

Drawing Schedule of deeds or documents, for each page of twenty-eight lines, cut post, . . | 0 | 3 | 4 |

Docket or Requisition for search in the Registry Office, for draft of five folios, or under, . . | 0 | 5 | 0 |

If more than five folios, for each folio from the commencement, ... | 0 | 1 | 0 |

Docket for search in any office, except the office of Registration of Deeds, including draft and one copy, ... | 0 | 3 | 4 |

Drawing necessary receipt and signing when no attendance charged, ... | 0 | 3 | 4 |

Drawing Case for Counsel, if less than six folios, . | 0 | 3 | 4 |

For each six folios or concluding part, . . | 0 | 3 | 4 |

ENGROSSMENTS :

Engrossing any document other than a deed or memorial, per folio, ... | 0 | 0 | 4 |

EXHIBITS :

Solicitor's fee for marking exhibits, for each exhibit, . | 0 | 0 | 6 |

FEES :

Term fee (no term fee will be allowed in the Land Commission Court).

Signing fee on any document requiring signature, . | 0 | 3 | 4 |

HAND SEARCH :

Fee for making hand search, if engaged for not more than one hour, ... | 0 | 6 | 8 |

If longer engaged, per hour, ... | 0 | 6 | 8 |

INSTRUCTIONS :

Ordinary instructions and instructions for briefs, apportionments, affidavits, objections, statements of facts, or to enter appearance, continuing proceedings in name of new party, ... | 0 | 6 | 8 |

To be increased according to circumstances, but not to exceed (save by direction of a Commissioner) . | 3 | 0 | 0 |

	£	s.	d.

LETTERS:

Writing letter, signing, and entry, ... 0 3 1

If several of same import, for each one after the first, . 0 2 0

LIS-PENDENS:

Fee on registering a lis-pendens (including stamp duty
and outlay), ... 1 0 0

Fee on registering every subsequent lis-pendens—
exclusive of outlay, ... 0 3 1

MARKING NAMES:

Marking the names of parties to be served on any
notice, etc., ... 0 3 4

MOTIONS EXPARTE:

Attending to fill up and lodge Exparte Motion docket, 0 6 8

Attending when motion heard, . . . 0 6 8

MOTION ON NOTICE:

Attending when Case in list and motion heard, . 0 13 4

If the Case lasts all day, ... 1 10 0

NOTICES:

Drawing special notice, ... 0 5 0

Or, at option of Solicitor, per folio, . . 0 0 9

Drawing a common notice, . . . 0 2 6

NEW SOLICITOR:

Fee to new Solicitor for reading documents and proceedings, ... 1 0 0

(To be increased under special circumstances by
permission of the Commissioner).

ORIGINATING STATEMENT:

Including all attendances and other business incident
to the preparation, lodgment, and verification of
same, including printing and scrivenery up to twenty
folios, but exclusive of the expenses of maps and
other necessary expenditure and travelling expense
where the purchase money does not exceed £500, . 3 3 0

Where the purchase money exceeds £500, . 4 4 0

If an Originating Statement is settled by Counsel
his fee must be certified for by a Commissioner.

PERUSALS:

Perusing and abstracting deeds for Abstract of Title,
for each skin of fifteen sheets, . . . 0 3 0

Not more than eight skins to be allowed for
any deed or Instrument. No fee for perusing a
document where the Solicitor has been paid for
perusing same within a period of two years prior
to the preparation of the Abstract.

Perusing or comparing any deed or instrument for
purposes other than the Abstract of Title, for each
skin, ... 0 2 0

	£	s.	d.

PERUSALS :—*continued.*

Perusing Bill of Costs by Solicitor opposing taxation,
for each 100 Items, ... 0 3 4
Perusing affidavits and statements of fact where
necessary, for each affidavit or statement, . 0 1 0
Or, at option of Solicitor, per folio, . . 0 0 3

POSSESSION :

Fee for attending for order to Sheriff to put purchaser
into possession, getting up order and lodging same
with Sheriff, ... 1 0 0

REQUISITIONS :

For filling, completing, and lodging requisition to have
order of a Commissioner reconsidered, . . 0 5 0
Drawing any other requisition, . . . 0 5 0

SEARCHES :

Fee and attendance on search for judgments, etc., and
for documents in any Public Office where made by
Officer, including attendance to bespeak, and for
search, where only one such search, . . 0 13 4
Where more than one such search, for each subsequent
search after the first, ... 0 6 8
Filling docket for search, . . . 0 3 4
Fee and attendance on search in the Registry of Deeds,
whether common or negative, made by Officer, . 0 13 4
If made by Solicitor, for each hour, . . 0 6 8
Not to exceed in one day, ... 1 0 0
Search by Solicitor for judgments or documents in
Public Office, for each hour, . . . 0 6 8
Not to exceed in one day, ... 0 13 4

SERVICE OF NOTICES OR OTHER DOCUMENTS NOT SERVED THROUGH NOTICE OFFICE :

In the City of Dublin, each person served, . 0 2 6
In the County of Dublin, or in any city or town other
than Dublin, ... 0 5 0
In other places, ... 0 10 0

SIGNING FEE :

Signing any document requiring signature, . 0 3 4

STATEMENT OF FACTS :

Drawing any statement of facts, . . 1 1 0
Or, at option of Solicitor, per folio, . . 0 1 6

TAXATION OF COSTS :

Drawing Costs for taxation, per item, . . 0 0 1
Attending to lodge and get day for taxation, . 0 6 8
Attending on taxation, for each 100 items, . 0 6 8
Preparing and engrossing Certificate of Costs, . 0 3 6
Or, at option of Solicitor, per folio, . . 0 0 4

PART II.

Costs of Vesting Order, including all attendances and other business incident to the preparation, lodgment, and completion of the same, including the completion of copies but exclusive of the necessary outlay, shall be as follows :—

	£	s.	d.
Where the total purchase-moneys of the holdings included in each Vesting Order shall not exceed £500, ...	3	3	0
If over £500 and not exceeding £1,000, .	4	4	0
If over £1,000 and not exceeding £2,000,	5	5	0
If over £2,000 and not exceeding £10,000,	6	6	0
If over £10,000, ...	10	10	0

And in addition in each case for the second and every additional holding included in a Vesting Order a sum of 5s.

www.ingramcontent.com/pod-product-compliance
Lightning Source LLC
Chambersburg PA
CBHW020803020726
47495CB00008B/2570